D1423347

For further information on Enid Blyton please visit *www.blyton.com*

ISBN 978-1-84135-430-9

ENID BLYTON ® Text copyright © 2012 Chorion Rights Limited
All rights reserved

Illustrations copyright © Award Publications Limited

First published by Sampson Low as *Enid Blyton's Holiday Book Series*

First published by Award Publications Limited 1993
This edition first published 2006

Published by Award Publications Limited,
The Old Riding School, The Welbeck Estate,
Worksop, Nottinghamshire, S80 3LR

12 5

Printed in the United Kingdom

# CONTENTS

# The Magic Clock

Once when Jinky went by Mother Goody's, he saw her nice round-faced clock.

Now Jinky had no clock, and he had always wanted one like Mother Goody's. He peeped in at the kitchen door. There was no one inside. Then the naughty little fellow ran to the mantelpiece, took down the clock, hid it under his coat and ran home.

"Mother Goody has two clocks, so she can spare me this one," said Jinky to himself. "But I'd better not put it on my mantelpiece in case anyone comes in and sees it. I will hide it."

So he put it in his larder. No sooner had he done that than Dame Fanny came in for a chat. Jinky gave her a chair and they sat talking away for a long time – but as they talked, a curious noise was gradually heard.

It was the noise of ticking – but, dear me, *such* loud ticking! "TICK-TOCK! TICK-TOCK! TICK-TOCK!"

"What's that noise?" said Dame Fanny, looking round in surprise.

"What noise?" said Jinky, going red,

and wondering whyever the clock ticked so loudly.

"That loud sort of tick-tock noise," said Dame Fanny. "I can't see a clock anywhere. It seems to come from your larder too – how strange, Jinky! What can it be?"

"Oh, just the cat in there, I expect," said Jinky, still very red. "Don't you think you ought to be going now, Dame Fanny? I believe I heard the bus coming!"

Dame Fanny jumped up in a hurry, forgetting all about the noise. She said goodbye and ran down the path. Jinky was glad to see her go. He went to the larder, opened the door and glared at the clock, which was now ticking softly again.

"You stupid thing!" said Jinky. "I suppose you thought you'd let Dame Fanny know you were here! Well, to punish you I'll take you upstairs to my bedroom and put you into the dark wardrobe. Then nobody can hear you ticking."

So he took the clock upstairs and put it into his wardrobe. He shut the door loudly. When he got downstairs he found his friend, Peter Penny, there.

"Hallo!" said Peter. "Can I have a drink of lemonade, Jinky? I'm so thirsty."

Jinky poured out a drink – and just as he was doing it, there came the sound of a bell ringing loudly. "R-r-r-r-r-ring, r-r-r-r-r-ring, r-r-r-r-r-ring!"

"Good gracious, what's that?" said Peter, jumping. He spilt the lemonade in his fright.

"Must be someone at the front door," said Jinky. But there wasn't anybody there. The bell rang again, even more loudly. "R-r-r-r-ring! R-r-r-r-r-ring!"

"Perhaps it's someone at the *back* door," said Peter Penny. But there was nobody there either.

Still the bell went on ringing and ringing. "Sounds like an alarm clock going off," said Peter, puzzled. "But you haven't got a clock, have you, Jinky?"

Jinky went red and didn't answer. Of

course, the noise was made by that tiresome clock! Still it went on ringing.

"I don't think I like it, Jinky," said Peter, getting up. "It's very strange – a bell ringing like that, and nobody at the door. Goodbye!"

Jinky tore upstairs to the clock, and took it out of the wardrobe. It stopped ringing and looked up at him with a cheeky round face. It waved its hands at him and then clapped them together.

"Tick-tock, I gave you a shock!" ticked the clock, and clapped its hands again.

"*You're* going to get a shock now," said naughty Jinky, and he took the clock down to the dustbin. He put it inside, and clapped the lid on it. "There! Now

the dustman can take you when he comes!"

But the clock didn't mind. It ticked loudly in the dustbin, it rang its bell as loudly as an ice-cream man's, and it jumped up and down against the tin lid of the dustbin, making a tremendous noise.

Mother Goody heard the noise as she passed by, and she called in at Jinky's window, "Jinky! There's such a funny noise in your dustbin. What have you got there?"

Jinky got such a shock when he heard Mother Goody's voice that he didn't know what to say. At last he stammered out, "Oh, it's only the c-c-c-cat, I expect, Mother G-Goody."

"The *cat*! In the *dust*bin! With the *lid* on!" cried Mother Goody in astonishment. "I never heard of such a thing! You just come and get that cat out, Jinky!"

She took Jinky by the collar and dragged him to the dustbin. She took off the lid – and there was her own round-faced clock staring up at her, ticking and ringing, and clapping its hands for joy!

"So *that* was what it was!" said Mother Goody. "I met Dame Fanny and Peter Penny this morning, and they both told me what funny noises they

heard in your house. I suppose you stole my clock, and when it wouldn't be quiet, you put the poor thing into the dustbin."

"Please forgive me," wept Jinky, very much afraid.

"Oh, I'll forgive you all right," said Mother Goody. "But I think you're a very rubbishy sort of person, Jinky – and rubbish goes into the dustbin, doesn't it? Well – in you go! Goodbye!"

And Mother Goody put Jinky into the dustbin, clapped the big lid over him, and taking her clock under her arm, went off home, smiling all over her face.

"He won't steal things again in a hurry!" said Mother Goody. "He'll have to stay there till the dustman comes this afternoon!"

"Tock-tick, tock-tick, what a very pretty trick," said the clock to Mother Goody. And you should have heard them both laugh!

# The Balloon
# in the Tree

Once there was a pixie called Winks who had a fine big blue balloon. He had got it at a party, and he was very proud of it indeed. It had a long string, and Winks took it with him wherever he went.

One day he went out with his balloon, and the wind blew so hard that it tugged the string out of Winks's hand. The balloon went up into the air, and flew straight into a tall tree. There it stuck, high up on a branch, wobbling a little whenever the wind blew.

"Oh!" cried Winks in dismay. "Come down, balloon! How silly you look up there! Come down."

The balloon took no notice of Winks at all. It just sat up in the tree and wobbled. Winks wondered if he could climb the tree and fetch it down. But it was much too hard a tree to climb.

"Oh dear! I can't lose my lovely balloon!" said Winks. "I really can't. I wonder what I can do to get it down."

Now just then who should come by but Mr Hobble with his stick. Winks ran up to him.

"Mister Hobble! Give me your stick for a minute! I want to get down my balloon."

He snatched away Mr Hobble's stick and ran back to the tree. But the stick wouldn't reach even half-way to the balloon. So Winks threw the stick up into the tree, hoping to move the balloon and make it float down.

But alas! The stick flew up and stayed in the tree. Its curved handle hung on a branch and there the stick swung, just by the balloon. Mr Hobble was very angry indeed.

"How dare you do that!" he cried. "You wicked pixie! If you don't get my stick down for me I will shake you till your teeth rattle like dice!"

Winks was frightened. Then he saw Miss Sally Simple coming along with a fine fat red umbrella. He ran up to her.

"Sally Simple! Let me have your umbrella for a minute. Mr Hobble's stick is stuck up in the tree and I must get it down for him."

He snatched at Sally's umbrella, and ran back to the tree. He sent the umbrella flying up into the branches to hit the stick down – but alas, it too stuck up in the tree, its handle swinging from a high branch!

Well, if Mr Hobble was angry, Sally Simple was even angrier. She shook Winks hard and cried, "If you don't climb up that tree and get down my umbrella I'll drop you splash into that pond over there!"

Winks began to cry. This was dreadful. Whatever was he to do?

Then he saw Mr Dig the gardener coming along, his spade over his shoulder. He ran up to him.

"Mr Dig, dear Mr Dig, lend me your spade to get down Sally Simple's umbrella from that tree!" he cried.

Before Mr Dig could say yes or no, Winks had snatched the spade from him and had run back to the tree. Up went the spade – crash into the tree. It didn't hit the stick. It didn't hit the umbrella.

16

It just broke two or three small branches – and then stayed high up in the tree, looking very peculiar there along with the balloon, the stick, and the umbrella!

"Now, look here, Winks, what in the wide world do you think you are doing?" cried Mr Dig angrily. "Are you making that tree into a Christmas tree and hanging it with presents for somebody – because that is what it is beginning to look like! Now just you get my spade for me, or I'll put you into that holly bush over there!"

Well, Mr Dig looked so fierce that Winks began to shiver and shake. He couldn't think *what* to do. And then he saw little Mrs Dot coming with her tennis-racket. She was on her way to a party. He ran up to her at once.

"Mrs Dot, be a pet and lend me your racket for a minute. I want to get Mr Dig's spade down from that tree. It's stuck up there."

"But how did it get up there?" asked Mrs Dot in great surprise. "My goodness – look at the things up there! Whatever's happened? Winks, you are not to throw my racket up into that tree. I forbid you to!"

But the racket had already gone! And there it stuck, of course, looking just as silly as all the other things. Mrs Dot was so angry that she went as red as the bow on her dress.

"Mr Dig! Sally Simple! Mr Hobble! How can you stand there and let Winks do these things? Here, take hold of one of his arms, Mr Dig. We'll send him up into the tree to fetch down our things! Now, are you ready – one – two – three – and *up* he goes!"

And up Winks went! My goodness, what a shock he got! He flew through the air right up into the tree and landed just by the spade. He wept bitterly and

18

pushed the spade off the branch. It fell down to the ground and Mr Dig went off with it.

Then Winks pushed down Sally's umbrella. She went off with that. Next, Mr Hobble's stick fell down, and after that Mrs Dot's racket. The two of them walked off, talking loudly about people who threw things up into trees.

"Hie! Come back and help me down!" yelled Winks, who knew quite well that he couldn't climb down by himself. But nobody paid the least attention to him and soon he was quite alone up in the tree. The wind came to have a look at him – and it blew the balloon right out

19

of the tree! Winks saw it flying down, down, down – and he saw the sandy rabbit come out of his hole to have a look at it. He saw the sandy rabbit nibble it to see if it tasted good – and he heard a loud POP and the balloon burst into bits! The sandy rabbit turned and fled for his life and didn't come out of his hole again for two days.

"There goes my balloon!" wept poor Winks. "Oh, dear, what an unlucky fellow I am! Whenever shall I get down from this horrible tree? Perhaps I shall be here all my life long!"

Well, he won't be – but he'll have to stay there until the evening when Mr Dig comes back from his work and will get a ladder to help him down. Poor Winks – he won't throw things up into trees again for a very long time!

# The Clockwork Steamer

John had a lovely clockwork steamer. It was blue, with red funnels, and although it wasn't very like the *Canberra*, John thought it was. So he called it the *Canberra*, and was very proud of it indeed. He used to wind it up and sail it in his bath every night. Chug-chug-chug-chug it went, and sailed up and down the bath, knocking into the sponge as it went. It looked great.

"Mummy, I wish I could sail it on the river," said John one day. "It doesn't get a proper chance in the bath. It's such a fine steamer, it ought to sail on something big, like the river or the sea."

"You would be silly if you did that, John," said his mother. "It would sail right away from you, and you might not get it back again."

"But, Mummy, I could take a stick with me and guide it," said John. "If it tried to get away I could pull it towards the bank."

"No, you mustn't sail it anywhere except in the bath," said Mummy.

Now John was not always obedient, and the more he thought about sailing his boat on the river the more he wanted to. And when he told his friend Emily about it, she longed to see it sailing there too.

"Bring it out this morning and we'll try it," said Emily. This was very naughty of her, because she knew John had been forbidden to do this. "We'll both take long sticks and then we can make sure the steamer will keep near the bank."

So John took his steamer to the river. He wound it up very full. He set it on the water. Chug-chug-chug-chug! it went. The children squealed with joy.

"Doesn't it look lovely! Oh, look at our lovely steamer!"

The steamer swung away from the bank. John tried to reach her with his stick, but she sailed away so quickly that he couldn't. He slipped – and fell into the river, splash! Emily screamed, and caught hold of his coat. She pulled him out, wet and muddy.

They both began to cry. "I'm wet and cold!" sobbed John. "And my steamer's gone!"

"Come home and get dry," said Emily. "We can't get the *Canberra* back. We oughtn't to have brought her. Now we shall be punished."

So two sad children went home, and the little steamer went chugging all by herself down the river. She was having a lovely time! This was better than the silly little bath!

"Chug-chug-chug-chug!" Along she went, and came to a family of ducks. "Chug-chug-chug-chug!"

The ducks saw the steamer coming towards them and they quacked in alarm.

"Quack! Quack! What is this creature coming to eat us? It has three red beaks sticking up. Quack! Quack!"

The steamer sailed straight at them and the ducks fled in fright. The steamer laughed in its chuggy voice. What fun it was having!

It sailed on, and soon came to where two moorhens were playing in the water. "Chug-chug-chug-chug!" said the steamer, and sailed straight towards them.

The moorhens heard it and looked round in alarm. "What is it?" cried one.

"A fish with three mouths sticking up!" cried the other. "Swim away quickly!"

They dived beneath the water and swam away to the opposite bank, only a ripple showing the way they went. The steamer was startled to see them disappear so suddenly, and it wondered what had happened to them.

On it went, enjoying itself tremendously. "Chug-chug-chug-chug! Chug-chug-chug-chug!"

It came to a family of frogs playing in the water. When they heard the toy steamer they looked round, and their big froggy eyes popped in alarm.

"It's a blue tadpole with three red tails sticking up!" cried a frog, and he dived under the water in alarm. All the others followed him, hoping that the strange creature would go away and leave them peace.

But the toy steamer stayed there. You see, her clockwork had run down, and she couldn't sail any more until she was wound up again. So there she floated on the water, no longer saying "chug-chug-chug-chug."

One by one the frogs popped up their heads and watched her. She seemed quite harmless.

"Do you know," said one frog, who was wiser than the rest, "I believe it's a boat. Let's go and tell the elf who lives on the bank over there."

So they swam to tell her, and she sat on a frog's back and rode to the steamer. She clambered on board and cried out in delight to see such a lovely steamer.

"Who will come and see over this fine ship with me?" she cried. Only one frog was brave enough, but he was fond of the little elf and climbed on board. She showed him everything – and then she leaned over and saw the key in the side.

"I believe if we turned that key round and round we could make this steamer go!" she said. "Oh, Frog! This boat is just what we elves want! We could use this steamer to take us from one side of the river to another. Some of us live on one bank and some on the other, and it such a nuisance to have to sit on a wet frog's back, with our legs in the water, whenever we want to visit one another! Shall we take this steamer for our own?"

They wound up the *Canberra* and the frog steered it from one side of the river to the other. The elf clapped her hands in joy.

"I shall make you a captain's cap and uniform," she said, "and you shall be captain of this ship. Will you like that?"

The frog was delighted. In a few hours the elf had made a smart, peaked cap, and a blue uniform with brass buttons all down it. The frog dressed himself up and got into the ship. The elf showed

him how to wind it up, and then he started on his new job as captain of the little *Canberra*!

And now you should see him every day, taking the elves to and fro in his steamer, looking as smart as can be in his cap and uniform. He says "Aye aye," instead of "Yes," whenever anyone speaks to him, so you can tell he is a real sailor now.

As for poor John, he never saw his steamer again – but if he ever tells you how he lost it, just show him this story, will you? I can't help feeling he would be rather pleased to know that his little steamer has a frog for a captain, and elves for her passengers every day of the week!

29

# Five
## Little People

There were once two children who hadn't been taught the right things by their father and mother. They were called Billy and Anne, and they were just a bit older than you are.

They hadn't been taught to tell the truth. They hadn't been taught not to touch what didn't belong to them. They hadn't even been taught such simple things as saying please and thank you, which even the tiniest babies learn.

So you can tell they were not very nice children. But it wasn't really their fault, because they hadn't been taught these things.

"The worst thing about those two children is that they take things that don't belong to them," said their next-door neighbour.

"I don't like Billy and Anne," said the teacher at school. "I can't trust them. I don't like to ask them to stay behind and do the flowers for me, because I know they will go off with a pencil out of someone's box, or a rubber from the store cupboard."

"I do wish Billy and Anne wouldn't take sweets out of my tin without asking me," said their granny. "It is very bad. I can't bear it. Whatever will they be like when they are grown-up, if they are so horrid now?"

Once Billy took a biscuit out of a tin at the grocer's. That was a really dreadful thing to do.

31

Once Anne went to tea, and when she went home she had with her one of the tiny dolls out of Hetta's dolls' house. She wanted it for her own, so she took it. Hetta asked her next day about it.

"Did you take my tiniest doll home by mistake, Anne?" she said.

"Of course not," said Anne at once, telling a very big story, for all the time that little doll was in Anne's bedroom at home.

Now, one day the two children went for a walk in the woods. They were lovely woods, thick and green, with all kinds of little paths about.

"Let's follow one we've never been along before," said Anne. So they chose a dear little winding path that led right into the heart of the wood. It was really a rabbit path, used by the rabbits every night and morning, but the children didn't know that.

It took them deep into the wood. No birds sang there. The trees pressed their green cheeks together and whispered loudly. The rabbits peeped from their

holes, and then scampered away under the ground.

"Isn't it quiet and strange!" said Billy, stopping. "Anne – look! Surely that isn't a house there – behind those trees?"

They both looked – and to their great surprise they saw a small white house set neatly in a little clearing among the trees!

It wasn't long before Billy and Anne were in the tiny garden, looking all round it! There was no smoke coming from the chimney. The curtains were drawn across the windows. There didn't seem to be anyone there at all.

Billy knocked at the door, but nobody came. He turned the handle. The door opened! The two went inside and looked round the dear, neat little house.

There were five beds in the bedroom, five chairs in the other room, five cups on hooks and five plates on the dresser. So five people must live there.

"Look!" said Billy in a whisper. "Five lovely red balls! Let's take one, Anne!"

So Billy slipped one of the balls into his pocket. Then Anne saw five little red bags hanging on pegs. She took one down and opened it. There was nothing inside except a clean blue hanky.

"I shall take this bag," she whispered to Billy. "I always wanted one like this."

Then they went to the larder. "There's an apple pie – and a jug of cream!" said Billy. "Do you feel hungry? I do!"

Well, those two naughty children ate the whole of the apple pie, and finished up all the cream. Then they opened a tin and found some lovely chocolate biscuits. They were in the middle of eating those when the door opened and five small people came in!

They were not brownies, they were not pixies and they were not goblins. They seemed to be a mixture of the three. They stared at the children in surprise.

"Why are you eating our biscuits?" asked one.

"Why have you eaten our apple pie and cream?" said another.

"Why have you taken a ball belonging to us, and a bag?" said a third.

"Is that the sort of thing that children do?" asked a fourth.

"Of course!" said Billy at once. "It doesn't matter taking somebody else's things at all. *We* haven't done wrong."

"We don't know much about your world," said the fifth little creature. "So you think it is right to take things belonging to someone else, do you? Please tell us, because we don't know."

The children thought the little creatures must be very stupid. They grinned at one another and said some very silly things.

"Oh, in our world nothing really belongs to anyone!" said Billy. "You can take anything you like, just as we have done here."

"It doesn't matter a bit," said Anne. "We are always doing that. All the same – I think we'll go now."

The children went off giggling. They

thought they had deceived the little people very cleverly. "How stupid they were!" said Anne, with a laugh.

But the little people were not so stupid as the children thought. They talked about it among themselves.

"If they can come and take *our* things, then we can go and take theirs," said the biggest one. "We will go tonight. We can tell where they live by following their tracks."

So that night the five little creatures trotted to the children's house, and made their way up an old apple tree into their bedroom. It was full of toys.

"I should like this big doll," said one.

"I should like this fine train," said another. The other three took a book, Anne's beautiful paint-box and Billy's school cap because it really was rather a grand one. Then they trotted off again.

What a to-do there was the next morning when the children found their things gone. "Where's my darling doll, Josephine?" cried Anne. "And my lovely paint-box?"

"And where's my train – and my book about dogs? And whatever has happened to my school cap?" said Billy.

He got into trouble for going to school without his school cap – but, no matter how he hunted, he couldn't find it. No wonder, because one of the little people in the wood was very proudly wearing it!

The next night the five of them were back again. "It's such a good idea to be able to take other people's things," said they. "What a good thing those children told us."

This time they hunted round a bit. One of them tried on Anne's school overall, which she had put ready to take the next day, because her class were having painting then. He liked it very much, rolled it up, and went off with it under his arm.

Another of them took Billy's slippers,

which fitted him nicely. They also took a picture from the walls, one of the chairs, and the big teapot. They were very pleased with themselves.

But Mother and the children were most amazed and puzzled next day. "Where's that chair?" asked Mother. "And who has taken down that picture? And, dear me, where's the big teapot? Children, what have you done with them?"

"Oh, Mother, nothing," said Anne. "*I* can't find my overall. And Billy's lost his slippers. It's very puzzling."

Mother thought the children had been playing silly tricks and she scolded them well. But no amount of scolding brought back the chair, the picture, the teapot, overall and shoes!

Next night the five little people came again. They thought it really was exciting to come and take anything they liked. They had decided that they must only take things from the children's house, not from anyone else's.

"It wouldn't be fair to take things

from people who hadn't taken anything from us," they said. "And, anyhow, there are plenty of things at the children's home."

So that night they rolled up the carpet and took that. They took down the curtains! They took Anne's dolls' house, and they took Billy's soldiers. They even took the clock off the mantelpiece, too!

Nobody could understand what was happening. "It's so strange," said Mother. "There's nothing gone anywhere except from the children's room. I simply can't understand it! If you two children are playing these tricks, I warn you that you will be well punished and sent to

bed! It isn't funny. It's very worrying."

The children were worried, too. They couldn't help wondering if the disappearances had anything to do with the five little creatures they had seen in the house in the woods.

"Let's watch tonight," said Billy. So they hid in the nursery cupboard and watched. And sure enough in at the window climbed the five little people from the wood!

Billy and Anne pounced out at them.

"You bad creatures! You wicked thieves! You robbers!"

The five little people glared at the two children. "What do you mean – calling us thieves and robbers! We are not! We have never been dishonest in our lives!

*You* told us it was quite all right to take things that belonged to somebody else!"

"*You* took *our* things!" said the biggest one. "So we are taking yours. Nothing could be fairer than that."

"It *isn't* fair," said Anne, beginning to cry. "You've got my lovely dolls' house – and my painting overall! You are perfectly horrid."

"It's your own fault," said the little people. "You told us we could. We are only doing what you did. You shouldn't have taken *our* things. We haven't got fathers and mothers to tell us what is right and wrong. We thought you knew what was good to do and what was not."

"But, if we are *really* doing wrong we will bring back all we have taken," said the biggest one. "But you must pay us

43

for the apple pie and cream, the chocolate biscuits, too, and give us back our ball and our bag."

The children emptied out their money-box and gave the little people all there was in it. They gave them back the lovely red ball, and the dear little handbag. The small creatures ran off, and presently came back carrying all the things they had taken.

And the next morning, when the children's mother saw everything in its place again, she was most astonished. "I knew you must have taken them away and hidden them for a silly joke!" she said, crossly.

The children told her about the little

44

house in the wood and all that had happened. But they had so often told naughty stories that their mother didn't believe them. Instead she put them to bed for a whole day.

"I haven't taught you to tell the truth, or to be honest and good," she said. "I thought you would grow up nicely without being scolded or taught. But you haven't. Now I see I have two horrid little children I can't trust. Well – it's never too late to mend!"

The two children cried bitterly that day. "I suppose we can't expect Mother to believe us when we do very often tell stories," said Anne. "Oh, Billy – don't let's take things that don't belong to us again. It's horrid, now we know what it feels like to have *our* things taken!"

It was a very good punishment for them, wasn't it? It's a good thing they hid in the bedroom and found out that it was the little people who were taking the things – or one day they wouldn't have had anything left at all!

# Giggle and Hop
# Get into Trouble

Dame Rap-Rap kept a school for pixies. It was a boarding-school, so they stayed there all the time, except when they went home for holidays. It was a very nice school and they all enjoyed it very much.

But there were two of the pixies who were real nuisances. If ever there was any trouble, Dame Rap-Rap was sure to find that it was because of Giggle and Hop. If the jam disappeared out of the cupboard, she would find that Giggle had been in the room two minutes before. If a window got broken, it would be because Hop had thrown his ball through it.

The worst of it was that it was very difficult to make sure that Giggle and Hop were the two that caused all the trouble. They looked so good and sweet that Dame Rap-Rap could really hardly believe they could be so naughty.

Now one night Giggle and Hop woke up and looked out of the window. It was a moonlight night and Giggle thought it looked beautiful.

"Hop! Let's go and watch the frogs playing leapfrog tonight!" said Giggle. "They are having their races. I heard Jump say so today, when we passed the pond."

47

"But we aren't supposed to go out at night," said Hop, half afraid.

"What does that matter?" said Giggle, jumping out of bed. "Everyone is asleep. No one will know. Let's go!"

So they both crept out of the window, slid down the tree outside, and set off to the pond. The frogs were there on the bank, having their jumping match. It was great fun to watch!

"You ought not to be out of bed at this time of night," said a big frog suddenly. "I shall tell Dame Rap-Rap."

"Mean thing!" said Hop, and both the pixies ran off in a hurry. The frog kept his word and told Dame Rap-Rap, and she was very cross.

"Now, which of you was it who went to the frogs' jumping-match?" she asked the school next day. Naughty little Giggle and Hop didn't say a word. They just sat at their desks, looking sweet and good. Dame Rap-Rap looked at them and felt perfectly certain it couldn't be either Giggle or Hop. So she didn't find out who it was at all.

Giggle and Hop thought it would be fine fun to slip out again one night. So when they heard the moths were holding a honey-supper in the wood,

they slipped out of bed, down the tree outside the window, and went to join the moths.

They were all sipping honey and telling each other the news. They flew softly here and there and their big plumy feelers waved to and fro as they chattered. Giggle and Hop tried to join in, and they each took a big pot of honey for themselves.

But the moths were angry.

"You haven't been invited!" they said. "Go home! You belong to Dame Rap-Rap's school, we know! We shall tell her tomorrow how you came here and took our honey. What are your names?"

But the pixies wouldn't tell the moths. They fled back to the school and went to bed. And in the morning Dame Rap-Rap had a letter saying that two of her pupils had slipped out the night before. She was very cross.

She simply *couldn't* find out who the naughty pixies were. Giggle and Hop just sat and looked as sweet as possible, and seemed quite shocked when Dame Rap-Rap said that SOMEONE had been out in the woods the night before.

Well, when they heard that the field mice were having a dance at the edge of the cornfield, they winked at one another and made up their minds to go there too, that very night.

So off they went, and weren't they pleased to see a fine spread of cheesecake, bacon rind sandwiches, and wobbly jellies set out for the fieldmice to eat. Giggle and Hop danced a dance together and then began to eat the cakes. They were really delicious.

They were just finishing a jelly when Pitter, the head fieldmouse, came scampering up. "What are you doing?" he cried. "You don't belong to our party! Go home! How dare you take our food!"

"We thought you would be proud if we came to the party," said Giggle. "It isn't often that pixies come to dance with the fieldmice!"

"You go home at once!" cried the fieldmouse angrily. "You go to Dame Rap-Rap's school, we know. Well, we'll tell her about you! You'll be punished!"

"Oh no, we shan't!" cried Hop, and he snatched another cake. The fieldmouse was so angry that he rushed at the pixie and knocked him right over. Then up came all the other fieldmice, and the pixies saw that they must run away.

They ran – but the mice ran after them! "Quick!" cried Giggle. "Hide!"

"Where?" cried Hop.

"In a poppy!" cried Giggle. The red poppies were standing here and there at the edge of the field. In a second the two pixies each climbed a green stalk, parted the red silky petals and hid themselves inside a poppy. The fieldmice raced along below and passed them, for they had not seen what the pixies were doing.

"Good!" cried Hop, when he saw that they were safe. "Come along! We'd better get back to school."

Off they ran, and were soon in bed. They didn't know that they were quite black with pollen off the poppies. You know what a black middle the poppies have, don't you? Well, all the black had come off on to the pixies!

They hadn't been in bed long when a fieldmouse came knocking at the school door. In great alarm Mrs Rap-Rap put on her dressing gown, and went down to open the door.

How angry she was when the fieldmouse told her that two of her pixies had been to the dance by the cornfield!

"Oh, really!" she said. "Well, I'll just find out this time who it is. I'll wake the whole school up and find out if everyone is here. Thank you, Fieldmouse!"

Dame Rap-Rap rang the school bell. All the pixies woke up in alarm. Dame Rap-Rap went in and out of the bedrooms calling, "Put on your dressing-gowns and go into the hall! Put on your dressing-gowns and go into the hall!"

In five minutes every pixie was there. Dame Rap-Rap counted them. Dear, dear! no one was missing after all. But then she looked very carefully at Giggle and Hop. They were *black!*

"Why are you so dirty?" she asked sternly. "Your faces are black, your hands are black – and dear me, your nightsuits, under your dressing-gowns, are black too! Have you been in the coal cellar?"

"No, Dame Rap-Rap," said the pixies at once.

"I know what the black is," cried little

55

Twinkle. "It's the black from the middle of poppies! I got some on my nose yesterday!"

"Oh!" said Dame Rap-Rap, and she stared sternly at the two trembling pixies. "And poppies grow by the cornfield – and the dance is held there tonight – and two pixies went – and were chased away and hid – and I guess they hid in the poppies and got black!

And I guess, too, that those pixies were *you*, Giggle and Hop! Come with me at once!"

They had to go with Dame Rap-Rap – and dear me, she hadn't got her name for nothing. All the other pixies stood and listened. "Rap-rap-rap!" they heard. "Rap-rap-rap!"

And if you'd like to get yourselves as black as Giggle and Hop, just go and put your nose inside a poppy. You'll soon see how it was that the pixies got so dirty!

# The
# Jumping Bean

Once Spink the pixie found a Jumping Bean in his garden. He was simply delighted.

You see, a Jumping Bean can jump on to anyone, and then they have to start jumping, too. It's very funny, if you happen to be watching – and Spink at once began to plan which people he would make jump.

"Chippy shall be the first!" said Spink. "He wouldn't lend me his umbrella yesterday."

So Spink went to meet Chippy, when Chippy came back from his shopping. "Jump, Bean!" he whispered. And as soon as Spink opened his hand the bean jumped out and landed somewhere on Chippy.

Well, of course, Chippy began to jump. He hopped down the street like a frog, most surprised. He couldn't walk. He couldn't run. He could only jump. It was very tiring and a great nuisance. Now he would have to jump all day.

"Come back, Bean!" shouted Spink. Then the bean jumped off Chippy, and bounded up the street to Spink. It jumped into his hand and he held it tightly. Chippy had heard Spink's shout, and he turned to him.

"Spink! You've got a Jumping Bean and you jumped it on me. Just you make me stop jumping!"

"Shan't!" said Spink, and he ran off. "Next time perhaps you'll lend me your umbrella!"

He soon met Dame Twiggle. "Jump Bean!" he whispered. "Dame Twiggle didn't ask me to her last party! She can do a little jumping!"

The bean jumped from Spink's hand to Dame Twiggle, and at once the old woman began to jump. She didn't like it at all. She wasn't used to jumping. She

liked to trot along with her umbrella.
She knew what had happened, and she
shouted to Spink:

"You bad pixie! You've got a Jumping
Bean. Stop me jumping at once."

"Shan't!" said Spink. "Now perhaps
you'll not leave me out of your party
another time! Come back, Bean!"

The bean came back – but Dame
Twiggle went on jumping, and jump she
would have to until the night came and

the magic wore off. Everyone stared at the strange sight of Dame Twiggle jumping along like a kangaroo, but the one who laughed most was unkind Spink.

"Now if only I could meet fat old Mister Tubby!" thought Spink. "It would do him good to hop along like a grasshopper! He gave me a slap last time he caught me taking plums from his trees. Ah – that looks like him coming round the corner."

It was. Spink grinned. "Jump, Bean!" he whispered, and the bean jumped high. It landed in the top of Mister

Tubby's grand new hat. And at once Mister Tubby began to jump.

How he jumped! He was a big fat brownie and he made a great noise, for his feet were big and he wore very large boots. Crash! Crash! Crash! People came running out of their houses to see what the noise was.

They couldn't help smiling to see poor Mister Tubby leaping along – but the fat brownie didn't smile. No, he didn't think it was at all funny. He was very angry indeed. He shook his stick at Spink, and roared at him, "I slapped you last week and I'll slap you again,

you bad fellow! Take this magic jumping from me at once."

"Not I!" cried Spink, and he held his sides because they ached with laughing. "It serves you right."

Mister Tubby jumped off down the road. "Come back, Bean!" cried Spink, and the bean came back. Spink held it in his hot little hand and thought of some more people he would like to make jump all day long.

He passed by Mrs Pippy's cottage. There was a most wonderful smell coming from her kitchen, for Mrs Pippy was a marvellous cook. Spink stopped and sniffed.

He liked Mrs Pippy, for she had once given him a taste of her new chocolate cake. He didn't want to make her go jumping all over the place. He wondered if she would give him a little of what smelt so very good – stew, or soup, or something, Spink thought it was.

So he went up the path and knocked at the door. Mrs Pippy opened it.

"Mrs Pippy, please will you give me

some of the stuff that smells so good?" said Spink, sniffing the air.

"Certainly not," said Mrs Pippy at once. She was a kind soul, but she didn't like people who came and asked like that.

"Mrs Pippy, you'd better give me what I want," said Spink. "I've got a Jumping Bean – and I'll jump it on to *you* if you're not careful!"

"You bad fellow!" said Mrs Pippy. "I

suppose it was your Jumping Bean that made poor Dame Twiggle go jumping by this morning – and Chippy, too. You've no right to use Jumping Beans to play jokes. They are meant to help lame frogs and grasshoppers, as you very well know."

"I don't care," said Spink, "I've had a lot of fun! Now, Mrs Pippy, what about that stew? Are you going to give me some or not? I'll jump the bean on to you if you don't, and you'll go hop-hop-hop for the rest of the day. And won't you be tired at night!"

Mrs Pippy opened the door wide. She had suddenly thought of something rather funny. "Come in," she said. "I'll give you some of the soup I am making. It's not stew."

"You're very sensible," said Spink. He sat down at the table, Mrs Pippy put a steaming hot plate of the most delicious bean-soup in front of him. Spink was so pleased! He put his Jumping Bean down on the table and took up his spoon. He turned to Mrs Pippy.

"This smells lovely," he said. He didn't notice what had happened when he turned to Mrs Pippy. His Bean had jumped straight into the plate of soup! Jumping Beans always jump to their brothers, if they come near them, and there were many beans in that plate of soup!

So, of course, Spink ate his Jumping Bean with all the other beans – and long before he had finished his meal his legs jumped him up from the table and sent him hop-hop-hopping round the room! He was angry and astonished.

"What's this?" he cried. "Where's that Bean?"

"You must have eaten it!" said Mrs Pippy with a giggle. "That was bean-soup, you see – and you know that Jumping Beans always jump to join their own kind. So it must have jumped into the soup, and you ate it!"

"You bad woman! You knew that would happen!" cried Spink in a rage, hopping about all over the place. "I've eaten it! I'll jump for the rest of my life!"

"Serves you right," said Mrs Pippy, opening the door and pushing him out. "Your Bean has done to you what you made it do to others. I hope you are enjoying it!"

But he isn't! He goes hop-skip-jumping along all day – and how he wishes he had never, never found that horrid Jumping Bean!

# The
# Lost Bus

Once when Miranda was going to school one day she missed the bus.

She saw it rumbling round the corner and she ran down the lane after it, crying bitterly. "Wait, wait! Wait, wait! Let me catch you. I shall miss school if I don't."

But the bus was gone. Miranda wasn't very old and she was very upset. She sat down on the grassy bank at the side of the lane and began to cry all over again.

"What's the matter?" said a voice, and a small man looked at her out of a rabbit-hole. "I've never heard anyone cry so much. What *can* be the matter? Can I help you?"

"No," said Miranda. "I've just lost my bus, that's all. You can't help me at all."

"Was it a nice bus?" asked the little man.

"Well – quite nice," said Miranda. "The usual kind."

"What colour?" asked the small man.

"Green and yellow," said Miranda, puzzled.

"How many wheels?" said the little fellow. "And did it have seats on the top as well as inside?"

"It had six wheels – and there are no seats on top," said Miranda, drying her eyes. "But what's the good of asking me all these questions? I tell you I've lost my bus and nothing you can do will bring it back. It's gone!"

"You wait!" said the tiny fellow. "My name is Tips and I've got a cousin called Tops. He's the guardian of all lost things. I may be able to get your bus for you."

He disappeared. Miranda was so surprised at all this that she didn't get up and go, but just sat there, wondering if the small man would come back.

He did come back. She heard a

curious clickety noise down the rabbit-hole, and looked into it. At first she could see nothing. Then she saw what looked like two little headlights.

"Parp-parp!" she heard, and up the rabbit-hole came a little green and yellow bus, tooting hard, driven by Tips! He was looking very pleased with himself. He drove right out of the hole and stopped the bus just beside Miranda. It was about the size of a toy bus.

He switched off the headlights. "It was so dark down the hole that I had to have the lamps on," he explained. "Well, here's the bus you lost. You said it had six wheels, but you made a mistake. It's only got four."

Miranda stared at the little bus and then at the proud little man.

"But I don't understand," she said. "Why have you brought me this dear little bus?"

"How stupid you are!" said the small man. "You said you had lost your bus, didn't you – a green and yellow one, with seats inside and not on top. Well, I went to my cousin, who takes charge of all lost things, and this was the only green and yellow bus that had been lost. So it must be yours!"

"But it *isn't*," said Miranda, and she began to laugh. "The bus I lost wasn't this one, really it wasn't. I lost the school bus."

"Lost the *school* bus!" said the little man, looking astonished. "But – how could you lose a great big thing like that? How very, very careless you are. I shouldn't have thought anyone would lose a great big bus like that."

"Oh dear. I don't mean I lost it like you lose money or a toy or something out of your pocket," explained Miranda.

"I was running to catch it to go to school – and it went without me. I was too late. I lost it."

"Oh," said the small man, looking very disappointed. "So that's what you meant. And you were crying your eyes out because of *that*! Well, well, perhaps I can help you after all."

He took a little tin from his pocket and rubbed himself with some yellow ointment out of it. At once he shot up as tall as Miranda. Then he rubbed the little bus.

"Gracious!" said Miranda. "The bus has grown enormous, too! I can even get into it!"

"Of course," said the small man – though he wasn't nearly as small now. "That's why I made it big. Get inside, little girl – and I'll drive you to school. It won't matter a bit if you've lost the other bus – you've got this one now!"

And will you believe it, he drove Miranda down the lane and out on the main road, and all the way to school at top speed! They actually caught up the school bus and passed it.

"Here you are," said the little fellow, stopping outside Miranda's school. "Out

72

you get. And don't lose any more buses! If you do, you know where to come for help! Goodbye!"

"Goodbye, Mr Tips," said Miranda, gratefully, and watched the funny bus speed away fast.

She went into school, feeling pleased and happy. What an adventure to have! She would go to that rabbit-hole the very next day and give Mr Tips a little present for being so kind.

But do you suppose she will know *which* rabbit-hole? There are so many there, you see, and she may not find the one that belongs to Mr Tips. I *do* hope she does, don't you?

# "Make-Haste"
# and "Be-Careful"

Once upon a time there were two gnomes who lived in cottages next door to each other.

Make-Haste lived in Apple Cottage and Be-Careful lived in Pippin Cottage. So you can perhaps guess by those two names that the gnomes grew plenty of apple trees in their gardens!

Make-Haste was just like his name – always in a hurry. Be-Careful was just the opposite. He liked to go slowly and make sure that he was doing the right thing. Make-Haste laughed at him.

"I've always got my washing done hours before you!" he would say.

"Ah, but mine is whiter when it's hung on the line!" Be-Careful would answer.

"I always finish my baking ages before you do!" Make-Haste would say.

"Yes, but my cakes taste nicer than yours because I spend more time in mixing them," Be-Careful would answer.

"Well, I don't care if your washing is a bit whiter than mine or your cakes are mixed more carefully!" Make-Haste would say. "I've much more time for reading and dancing and going out to parties than you have!"

Now, one year the apple trees in the two gardens were so loaded with fruit that some of the trees had to be propped up with posts, or the boughs would have broken.

"Did you ever see such a crop?" said Make-Haste to Be-Careful.

"Never," said Be-Careful. "We shall make a lot of money by selling our apples about Christmastime, when people want fruit to eat."

"It will be fun to pick them," said Make-Haste.

"It will take a very long time," said Be-Careful. "There are so many to pick!"

"Pooh – it won't be a very long job!" said Make-Haste. "You always think everything will take a long time. I suppose you are going to polish every apple before you put it away, or something like that!"

"No, I'm not," said Be-Careful rather crossly. "I'm not so silly as that. But I do know that it would be stupid to hurry over the picking of our beautiful apples

if we want them to keep until Christmas."

Well, when apple-picking time came the two gnomes set to work on the same day. At the end of the day Make-Haste had picked six of his biggest trees. Be-Careful had only picked the apples off three.

"My dear fellow, what *have* you been doing?" said Make-Haste in surprise. "You *are* slow! You've only picked half the number of apples that *I've* picked!"

"Well, I've picked them carefully," said Be-Careful. "You just pick yours anyhow,

77

and tumble them into the basket and tumble them out on to the floor of your loft. Apples don't like being treated like that. You'll be sorry when Christmastime comes, because mine will be better than yours."

"Oh, you always say things like that," said Make-Haste. "Always making excuses for your slowness."

"They are not excuses," said Be-Careful, annoyed. "They are very good reasons. You don't know the difference between a reason and an excuse!"

Now, the next day the two gnomes had a letter each, and a very exciting letter it was, too. It was an invitation from Mr High-Up to come to his birthday party.

"I say! That will be fun!" said Make-Haste. "I shall buy myself a new coat and a new hat and a new pair of shoes."

"You haven't got any money," said Be-Careful in surprise.

"Ah, but I shall have plenty at Christmastime when I sell my apples!" said Make-Haste. "I shall go to the shop

78

and tell them I will pay at Christmastime. They will wait for their money."

"You know you shouldn't do that," said Be-Careful. "You should pay your bills at once and not make people wait for their money. I shall go in my old clothes and that's what you ought to do, too."

"Oh, you're always so good and careful!" said Make-Haste.

"Well, if you badly want to buy new things, why don't you sell some apples now and get the money?" said Be-Careful.

79

"Because I want to keep them until Christmas, when I shall get double the price for them," said Make-Haste. "You know that quite well. Now I'm going on with my apple picking. I shall have to hurry because I want to go down to the village and order my new clothes."

He did hurry. He hurried so much that he picked his apples and threw them into his basket twice as fast as Be-Careful. Some of them fell to the ground and were bruised. They all went into the loft, higgledy-piggledy!

By the time the afternoon came Make-Haste had picked every one of his apples. He was very pleased. He looked over the wall and saw that Be-Careful hadn't finished half his trees.

"Your second name is Slow-Coach!"

80

he called. "I've finished. I'm off to the village to order my new clothes. Good-bye, Slow-Coach."

He went off. Be-Careful picked all the afternoon and evening, pulling each apple off its stalk, and placing it very carefully and gently into the basket. When the basket was full he took it to his loft and, picking out the lovely red apples one by one, he put them carefully in rows on the floor. Not one apple was allowed to touch another. "Then, if one goes bad, it won't make its neighbour go bad too," said Be-Careful.

Now, when Christmastime came, Mr High-Up sent to say that he would buy all the apples that Make-haste and Be-Careful had, and would pay them ten pence a pound. The two gnomes were simply delighted.

"We shall make a lot of money!" said Be-Careful and he went up to his loft to weigh out his apples. They looked lovely, and they smelt lovely too. Not a single one was bad. Be-Careful had put aside any that were bruised or pecked, and he had picked them so carefully that every apple was perfect now.

But from Make-Haste's cottage there came groans and sobs, and Make-haste rushed into Be-Careful's cottage.

"Every one of my apples is bad! Oh! Look at yours, so beautiful and perfect.

Why are mine bad? They are just a big, rotten, horrid-smelling pile in the loft. And, oh dear – I owe all that money for my clothes, and I shan't have any to pay."

"Make-Haste, I'm sorry for you," said Be-Careful. "You really do know that you should pick apples carefully and not let them fall, or get bruised. It's your own fault for being in such a hurry."

"I know, I know. I'll be careful in future," wept Make-Haste. "Please will you lend me some money?"

"Yes – but you must come and work in my garden for me until your debt is paid," said Be-Careful. "And mind, Make-Haste, you will have to work *my* way, and not yours!"

So poor Make-Haste is now working in Be-Careful's garden for him – and dear me, what a lot he is learning. Be-Careful says he will give him another name soon – a much better one. He says he will call him "Slow-but-Sure."

Well – it's a better name than "Make-Haste," isn't it?

# Mr Gobo's
# Green Grass

There was once a funny little man called Mr Gobo. He lived in Twisty Cottage, and he had a nice little garden.

How he loved his green grass lawn! He wouldn't let a single daisy grow there. He pulled up every bit of clover. He even drove away the worms, and poured boiling water on any little brown ant he saw hurrying over the lawn.

"The Prince of Ho-Ho is coming to see me this summer," he told everyone. "And I am going to give him tea on my lawn. There mustn't be a single weed there, or a single worm or insect. No, not one!"

He set his little servant to work each day on the lawn. The servant was small and thin, and her name was Tiny. She had to pull the heavy roller over the grass two hundred times each day to make it smooth and even. She had to cut the grass with the lawn-mower twice a week. She had to sweep away any worm-casts that dared to show themselves in the morning.

Tiny was very tired of Gobo's beautiful green grass. She leaned over the fence and talked to the maid next door about it.

"I like the field grass," she said. "It has tiny flowers growing in it. It has ants and spiders and bright little beetles

hurrying through it on their busy ways. I don't like Mr Gobo's lawn. It breaks my back when I have to roll it each day. If only he would do it himself!"

But Mr Gobo wouldn't do any of the hard work himself. No – Tiny must do that. He would pour hot water on a hurrying ant, or stamp on a poor worm, or pull up a small daisy – but Tiny must roll and cut and sweep.

The lawn was really beautiful. It looked like a piece of green velvet. Gobo

grew more and more proud of it.

"I can't imagine what the Prince of Ho-Ho will think when he sits on it to have his tea," he boasted. "I am sure he has no grass as beautiful as mine. Well, he may have his palace, his hundred rooms, his golden plates – but I have a better lawn than he has!"

"But what's the use of your lawn?" asked Jinks, his next-door neighbour. "You never play games on it. You never let your dog have a run round it. You even chase your soft-footed cat off it!"

"I should think so!" said Gobo. "And let me tell you this, Jinks – *your* cat was stamping about on my beautiful lawn yesterday! If you don't stop her doing that, I'll shoot peas at her from my pea-shooter."

"Don't you dare to do anything of the sort," cried Jinks fiercely. "I love my cat, and I won't have her hurt!"

As the day drew nearer for the Prince of Ho-Ho to come and visit him, Gobo grew more and more careful of his lawn. He shooed the birds off it. He killed every worm he found. Not an insect dared to fly over it.

Once his dog forgot, and ran lightly over the smooth green grass. Gobo was so angry that he whipped his dog till the poor dog cried.

He shot at Jinks' cat with his pea-shooter the next time it dared to walk on his lawn, and the cat bounded off in fright.

Tiny had to work with the roller and the broom till she was tired out. Up and down the lawn she went, up and down in her rubber-soled shoes, till she never wanted to see a roller, a mower, or a broom again.

The day before the prince's visit came, Gobo stood in his garden and looked proudly at his lawn. It was perfect. He was simply delighted with it. How envious the Prince of Ho-Ho would be! And how proud Gobo would feel when the prince admired his lawn!

Suddenly, as he stood there, two cars came by his gate. A dog ran across the road in front of them; they both swerved to the middle of the road to save the dog – and CRASH! They bumped into one another!

"Oh dear, oh dear!" cried a voice from

one car. "This is such a shock! I think I shall faint!"

It was little Mother Tickles, who drove her car very carefully, because she was so afraid of accidents – and now she had had one! Her cheek was cut by the flying glass of her broken windscreen. She looked very pale indeed.

Mr Curly was in the other car. He jumped out at once and hurried to Mother Tickles in dismay. "Now, now! Don't faint or do anything silly!" he said. "You are not really hurt. Come along into this garden here, and I'll get some water to bathe your cheek."

He hurried Mother Tickles into Gobo's garden gate, and made her sit down on the lawn. He shouted to Gobo, "Bring some water! There's been an accident!"

"Please get off my grass," said Gobo, horrified to see anyone on his precious lawn. "Get on to the path."

"Don't be silly," said Mr Curly crossly. "The grass is soft to sit on. We shan't hurt it. Get some warm water."

Gobo was very angry. He ran up to Mother Tickles, pulled her off the grass, and sat her down hard on the dusty path. "How dare you use my grass!" he shouted.

Jinks next door saw and heard all this. He was shocked. He called to Mr Curly, "Bring Mother Tickles into my garden. *I'll* fetch some water and a towel."

So poor Mother Tickles was taken into Jinks' garden and he bathed her cut cheek and looked after her. Gobo glared at them over the fence, and then went to see if his beautiful lawn had been hurt.

"You know, Mr Gobo wants a good lesson," said Mr Curly, looking at the grass next door. "Spending all his time making quite a useless lawn just to make the prince envious! Can't even let poor Mother Tickles sit down on it! The wretch!"

"Yes," said Jinks slowly, looking at the grass next door. "He *does* need a lesson. You're right! And he'll get it too, before the Prince of Ho-Ho comes! Yes, he'll get it all right!"

When Mother Tickles and Mr Curly had gone, Jinks put on his hat and went to Tibby Lickle, who was a funny old woman living alone on the hill. She knew every creature of the woods and fields, and could talk to them as easily as she could talk to Jinks.

"Tibby Lickle," said Jinks, "I want something done."

"And what's that?" asked old Tibby Lickle, her bright green eyes twinkling up at Jinks. "I'll do anything for *you*, Jinks. You're a good kind fellow. That I know!"

"Well, Tibble Lickle, what I'm asking you to do will not seem kind," said Jinks, "but it needs to be done. Now, I want you to go the moles, who live under the ground, and ask them to tunnel up and down beneath Mister Gobo's lawn tonight. Will you do that?"

"Indeed I will," said old Tibby Lickle, and she went straight off to give the message.

And that night six velvety moles tunnelled underground till they came to Gobo's beautiful lawn. And then, all night long they tunnelled below his grass, making passages underneath it, up and down, up and down. Here and

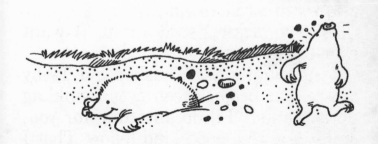

there they threw up hillocks of fine
earth on the grass. How those moles
worked – and then they slipped away
silently along their underground
passages.

And when Gobo awoke next morning
and looked out of the window, *what* a
shock he got! His lawn was completely
spoilt! It was bumpy and uneven, where
the moles had tunnelled beneath it. It
was covered with hillocks of earth. It
wasn't a lawn at all!

"Oh! Oh! Look at that!" he wept.
"Tiny, where are you? Oh, look at
that!"

Tiny stood and looked at the lawn.
"Ah, master," she said, "you wouldn't let
an old woman sit on your precious lawn

yesterday – and now it is spoilt! It serves you right! Whatever will the prince say?"

The prince came – and how he did turn up his nose at poor Gobo's spoilt lawn!

"Dear me!" he said. "You must take a few lessons from one of my gardeners, Gobo! This is dreadful! How you have let your lawn go to pieces!"

"I don't need any lessons," said Gobo, his face very red. "I've had one big lesson – and that's quite enough for me! In future my lawn isn't going to be beautiful – it's going to be useful!"

And so it is. The dog plays on it, the cat washes herself there, the birds fly down to it, and the worms have a fine time. What could you want better than that?

# The
# Monkey's Tail

Tickles, the pixie, came to play with the toys as usual one night, but she didn't look very well.

"What's the matter?" said the teddy-bear. "You do look down in the mouth."

"I don't feel very well," said Tickles. "I think I'm going to get a cold. A-tish-oo!"

"Well, don't give it to me then!" said the doll in the blue silk dress. "I don't want to be in bed, sneezing my head off."

"It wouldn't matter if you did," said the toy clown rudely. "It's a silly sort of head – no brains at all!"

The doll smacked him. "Oh, don't," said Tickles. "I do want a bit of peace tonight. I like you, toys, but you really are a quarrelsome lot, you know! Only the old monkey is really unselfish and peaceful."

"Pooh! Old Monkey!" said the ragdoll. "He's falling to bits! Look at his tail – hanging on by a thread, and very dirty indeed."

"Well, I couldn't help falling into the coal scuttle," said the monkey. "I've managed to clean myself up a bit, but somehow my tail won't come clean – and I daren't do too much to it in case it falls off."

"Never mind, Monkey. I think you're lovely," said Tickles. "Let me lean against you tonight. I do feel so tired. My throat hurts so, too."

The toys were bored with Tickles because she wouldn't play with them. So they went off by themselves. Tickles sat with Old Monkey, and he made himself just as soft a cushion for her as he could.

"It's time for me to go," said Tickles at last. "Oh dear – it's cold, isn't it! And I haven't got a coat tonight. Or even a scarf."

"Well, the doll will lend you her coat," said Monkey. "And Rag-doll will you lend you his scarf. He's got a nice one."

But they wouldn't lend her either a coat or a scarf. Weren't they horrid! "She'll only get my coat wet in the rain," said the doll. "It's just begun to pour."

"And I'm certainly not going to lend anyone my scarf," said the rag-doll. "I look awful without it!"

"Well, never mind," said Tickles. "I'll go home as quickly as ever I can and get straight into bed."

"I'll tell you what I can do," said Old Monkey. "I can lend you my long, soft tail for a scarf, if you don't mind it being a bit dirty."

"But you can't pull your tail off for me!" cried Tickles. "A monkey without a tail! Why, I never heard of such a thing. Suppose the children you belong to saw you without your tail? They wouldn't want you any more. And I might not be able to bring it back for a little while, because I'm sure I shall be in bed for a few days."

"Never mind," said Old Monkey. He took hold of his tail, gave a pull, and snapped the few threads still holding it to his body. He shook the dust from it and then wrapped it round and round

Tickle's throat. He tucked the ends into her belt. "There you are!" he said. "That will keep you warm and cosy."

"Oh, it's lovely!" said Tickles, pleased. "You *are* kind. I love you, Monkey. Goodbye. I'll come and see you when I am better."

She flew off and the toys gathered round Monkey. "You look awful without a tail," said the doll.

"I'd feel worse if I were like you and hadn't got a heart!" said Monkey.

"You're rude," said the doll. "I hope the children find you without a tail and throw you away!"

Monkey was rather afraid of that himself! He knew that a monkey without a tail didn't really look a proper monkey. He hid himself right at the very back of the toy cupboard and hoped the children wouldn't see him.

A day passed and then another. Then a third came and passed. Monkey began to be worried – not so much about his tail, as about little Tickles. Was she very ill?

Then on the fourth night she came again, all smiles. "I'm quite better," she said. "I only took two days in bed. On the third day I had to go and visit the Princess of the Silver Mountain. She's giving a birthday party and I'm in charge of all the arrangements. Fancy that! And I can ask one guest of my own to come."

"Oooh. Do ask *me*!" said the doll.

"No, me," said the rag-doll.

"Where's old Monkey?" asked Tickles. "I can't see him anywhere. Don't tell me that the children have thrown him away after all!"

"Here I am," said the monkey, coming out of the cupboard. "Oh – you've brought back my tail. Thank you!"

"I *was* glad of it," said Tickles. "Look, I've washed it nice and clean – it's beautiful now, isn't it? And I've brought some soap and flannel to wash all your fur clean, Monkey. And look, here is a needle and cotton to sew on your tail again – I won't hurt you a bit."

"Oh, thank you," said Monkey. "What's that blue thing you've got there?"

"It's a blue ribbon to tie round your neck in a smart bow," said Tickles, beginning to wash Monkey all over with flannel and soap. "It's for *you*!"

She soon had him looking very clean and smart. She sewed on his long tail. Then she brushed his fur and tied the blue bow round his neck.

"All dressed up and nowhere to go!" said the ragdoll with a laugh.

"Oh - he's got somewhere to go all right!" said Tickles. "He's coming to the princess's birthday party with me tonight. Didn't I tell you? Come along, Monkey. I've got a little golden carriage outside, especially sent for us, drawn by six white mice. It's very grand."

So it was. Monkey could hardly believe it when he found himself sitting in such a grand carriage, a blue bow under his chin, ready to set out for the

Silver Mountain. Well, well – what a very astonishing thing!

The toys watched them go. They were very quiet.

"You know, I think he deserves all this," said the teddy-bear suddenly. "He really is a good, kind fellow."

"Yes," said the ragdoll in a small voice. "We'd better be kinder ourselves in future. I do really think we had."

I think so, too. I would have liked to see Tickles wearing Monkey's tail for a scarf, wouldn't you? It really was a very good idea.

# Shut
# The Gate

"Hey, you there! Shut the gate, can't you?" roared a voice. Pat and Biddy turned round. A big man was standing in a field by the lane, pointing with his stick at the gate they had left open behind them.

Pat ran back and shut the gate. Biddy felt scared when the big man came out of his field and walked up to her.

"Hasn't anyone ever told you to shut gates behind you?" he said, crossly. "Haven't you got enough brains to shut them yourselves even without being told?"

"We *have* been told," said Biddy, going red. "I'm sorry we forgot. Does it matter very much?"

"Matter very much?" roared the

farmer, his voice very loud again. "Now, you use your common sense! What keeps those horses in the field? What keeps my sheep from wandering into the road? What stops those calves over there from running out and getting lost or knocked down?"

"The gate," said Pat, scared. Biddy couldn't say a word. She wanted to run away.

"Yes, the gate," said the farmer.

106

"What are you doing in my fields, anyway?"

"Well, we're very fond of animals," said Pat. "We love horses, and we like cows. Biddy loves the little calves, and we like going to watch the lambs frisking about. Does it matter going into the fields to talk to them?"

"Not if you always shut the gates behind you," said the farmer. "I like to see children fond of animals – but I don't like to see them letting horses and cows run the risk of getting loose in the road, and maybe knocked down by a car. You mind what you're doing!"

He walked off. Pat and Biddy went home without saying a word. They felt very guilty. Uncle Ben and Auntie Sue were always warning them about shutting gates – yes, and doors, too. If the kitchen door or any other door was left open the hens and ducks walked in.

It was lovely staying in the country with Auntie Sue. It was glorious to wake up in the morning and hear the hens clucking just outside the window,

the ducks quacking on the pond nearby and the clop-clop of horses' hoofs in the yard. It was much, much better than being in a town.

Pat and Biddy loved every single bird and animal round about. They even loved the big old sow, and they adored her nine baby pigs. But perhaps most of all, they loved Bray, the donkey.

He was grey, with long ears and a tail that swished the flies away very cleverly. He had a way of coming sideways up to the children, rubbing himself against them and putting his big grey nose on to their shoulders.

108

"He likes us as much as we like him," said Biddy, in delight. "I'm going to save my lumps of sugar for him each day instead of putting them in my cocoa."

"And I shall bring him a carrot if Uncle will let me," said Pat. "And I shall brush him and clean him just as if he was a horse."

Bray gave them rides. He cantered with them and even galloped once or twice, which felt very grand and exciting. The children went to see him as often as they could, and whenever he saw them coming he trotted to the gate to meet them.

"I wish he was ours," said Pat. "He's not, but he does seem to belong to us two, doesn't he, Biddy?"

"Yes, he does. Shan't we miss him when we go back home!" said Biddy.

"Pat, let's ask Uncle if we can borrow his camera and take a picture of him, shall we? I'd love a photo of Bray to take home."

Bray used to have a little donkey-cart to draw along, but now he was old and he didn't do anything except have a good time in the field, and talk to the horses when they came back from work at night.

"But he doesn't really *seem* old, does he?" said Pat to Biddy. "He canters and brays and he's not a bit patchy in his coat, like some old animals are."

Uncle Ben and Auntie Sue were amused at the way the children fussed over Bray.

"Yes, he's a nice old thing," said Uncle Ben. "But he's been a rascal in his time. There was a year when he kept getting through the hedge and wandering into people's gardens and doing a lot of damage. We really thought he did it out of mischief! He had a lot of beatings then."

"*Beatings!*" said Biddy in horror. "Did

you ever beat dear old Bray? Oh, poor thing! But you won't ever beat him again, will you, Uncle?"

"I shouldn't think so," said Uncle Ben, smiling. "Dear me, Biddy, is that sugar for Bray again? No wonder he loves you so much!"

Bray and the horses lived in a field quite near to the house. You had to go up the garden, out of the little gate at the top, up the lane a little way and then through the big five-barred gate into the field. And, at the gate waiting for them would be Bray, his long, grey nose over the top bar, his eyes looking for them down the lane.

One day they were not allowed to go and see Bray. Auntie Sue was very cross with them. "Just look!" she scolded, standing in their bedroom. "Clothes on the floor – the card game you were playing last night still scattered all over the place – your beds not made – every cupboard and drawer left open! I will not have such carelessness and untidiness. Now you begin straightaway and clear up. And sew that button on your jacket, Biddy. Oh, yes, you *can* sew it on all right, even if it *is* a bit stiff to get the needle through the thick material. And you take your dirty, muddy boots down to the yard and clean them at once, Pat. If you are going to walk in all the mud you can find, you can clean them yourself!"

The children stood sulkily in the bedroom. Bother! Blow! They were just going to see Bray.

Auntie Sue knew that. "You won't see that donkey of yours at all today," she scolded. "All you think about is rushing off here, there and everywhere and doing exactly what you like without ever thinking of the trouble you give anyone else. I've a good mind to send you back home."

This was a terrible threat! Holidaying

in the country with dogs and hens and horses, and cows and sheep, and dear old Bray was much better than being in a crowded town. The two children began to clear up at once.

Auntie Sue spoke to Uncle Ben about them. "I don't know how to make those two pull themselves together and try to remember the things they must do, Ben. They are nice children but *so* spoilt. They're forgetful and careless, and yet they never get into mischief like some children do."

"They'll learn one day," said Uncle Ben. "Something will teach them. You'll see!"

"Well, I wish whatever it is would hurry up and come, then," said Auntie Sue. "I'm tired of always running round after them."

The children didn't see Bray that day. He stood by the gate waiting, but they didn't come. He was sad and the children were sadder still. "We'll go tomorrow," said Biddy. "I shall have lots of sugar to take him. Poor Bray. He will be feeling so lonely today."

They set off to visit him after breakfast the next day. They had remembered to make their beds and put away their things. Bray was waiting for them at the gate. He gave a loud "He-haw" of welcome.

"He sounds as if he's laughing for joy," said Pat. "Good old Bray."

They were soon petting the old donkey, and then they rode him round

the field. They quite forgot the time, and when the church clock struck twelve they slid off Bray's back in horror.

"Twelve o'clock! And Auntie told us to be back by eleven o'clock sharp to go and do some shopping for her!" They rushed back to the house. Auntie Sue was just beginning to feel cross. Those children!

They had been in such a hurry that they hadn't shut the field gate. They hadn't even shut the garden gate! And they left the kitchen door open behind them, so in walked two hens, a duck and three chicks. Auntie Sue shooed them out and banged the door.

"Why you can't remember even such a simple thing as shutting a door, I don't know," she said. "There is the shopping list – there is the basket – and here is the money. Go along before I find myself getting cross with you again, and PLEASE SHUT THE DOOR BEHIND YOU!"

They did. They scurried off to the village at top speed. Oh dear – how

difficult it was to remember everything they were told to do!

They did all the shopping and made their way back home. As they drew near they heard some very peculiar sounds. Shouting, yelling, galloping, thuds and crashes! Gracious, whatever could be happening?

They ran to see – and they stood still in horror and grief. Uncle Ben and two men were hitting Bray, yelling at him,

and Bray was cantering madly about the garden, with hens scuttling away from his hoofs.

Pat and Biddy flung down the shopping and rushed to their uncle. "Don't! Don't! Why are you hitting poor Bray like that? Oh, you're hurting him. DON'T, Uncle, DON'T!"

Bray crashed into a frame of cucumbers and Uncle Ben gave him such a whack with a stick that the donkey leapt into the air with fright. One of the men tried to catch him, but Bray ran the other way, right across the bed of roses that Auntie Sue loved so

118

much. Biff! Uncle Ben hit him again.

Biddy was crying desperately. Pat tried to hang on to his uncle's arm to stop him hitting Bray again, but his uncle, who was in a furious temper, shook him off. "Get away, you stupid boy! If I don't get this donkey out of here, he'll ruin every flower and vegetable your aunt has grown this year!"

Suddenly Bray ran out of the garden gate and up the lane. One of the farm men chased him. Pat and Biddy wanted to go, too, and comfort Bray, but Uncle Ben took hold of them and led them indoors. They were both crying bitterly. "You cruel, unkind man!" sobbed Biddy. "I'll never like you again. I wish you weren't my uncle!"

Auntie Sue stood by the window staring out at her ruined flowers, spoilt lettuces and rows of radishes, and the broken frames. She looked sad.

"That donkey!" raged Uncle Ben. "I'll get rid of him! I'll sell him tomorrow! Going back to his old tricks again – well, he's had a good thrashing, anyhow!"

"How did he get here?" asked Auntie Sue. "I suppose his field gate had been left open by some walker or other – and our garden gate must have been left open, too."

Pat felt his heart suddenly sink down into his boots. The gates! Why, he and Biddy hadn't shut them behind them when they had run off at twelve o'clock in such a hurry. Bray must have got out

– and come to look for Biddy and Pat, his friends. And what did he find? Men yelling and shouting at him, men chasing him and hitting him with sticks. And now he would be sold, and have to live in a place he didn't know and with people he probably wouldn't like. Pat gave such a gulp that Biddy looked at him in surprise.

"Uncle! Don't sell Bray! It was our fault – we left the gates open!" he said. "He came to look for us – he didn't mean to do any damage! I expect he got frightened when you yelled at him, and then he galloped about. Oh, Uncle, please, please don't sell him."

His uncle looked at him grimly, and then at Biddy. "So *you* left the gates open – after all you've been told! And because of you the garden is ruined and Bray has been beaten, and may be sold. I hope you feel pleased with yourselves. Careless, spoilt children! Nothing will teach you to pull yourselves together and be a bit responsible. I shall sell Bray tomorrow."

He got up and went out, still angry. Auntie Sue looked at the two unhappy children sadly. "I'm afraid Bray *will* be sold," she said. "It's dreadful to think he will have to leave his home, when he is so old, all because of you two." The children couldn't eat any dinner at all. They went out into the ruined garden. Pat began to try and put things straight. "We'll do what we can," he said to Biddy. "We simply must. I feel awful."

They worked hard for three hours. They rolled the lawn to level out Bray's hoof-marks. They rolled the paths. They raked over the prints he had made in

the beds. They tied up broken plants. Pat took all the money out of his money-box to pay for the broken frame. He felt as if he would never smile again.

Auntie Sue must have said something to Uncle Ben about it, because he didn't look nearly so cross at teatime. The children hardly dared to say a word. But at last Pat screwed up enough courage to ask a question.

"When are you going to sell Bray? Please, Uncle, may we come with you and see who you're going to sell him to? We – we want to say good bye to him, you see. We want to explain things to him."

"Now, you listen to me," said Uncle Ben seriously. "I'm not going to sell Bray, because your aunt tells me you've

been trying to put right the damage that has been done because of you – and also because I'm going to give you one more chance. You won't forget in a hurry how horrible it is to see somebody else suffering because of a silly thing *you've* done, will you?"

"Oh, no – we'll never, never forget," said Biddy, tears coming into her eyes when she thought of poor Bray being hit so hard. "Uncle, give us another chance. We'll go and tell Bray we're sorry he was hurt, and we'll tell him that because he was hurt we'll never do silly things again."

"All right!" said her uncle gruffly. "You can go and see your precious donkey now. And take him this apple from me!"

So off they went as fast as their legs would take them. Do you suppose they kept their word? Well, if a thing like that happened to *me*, I'd never forget my promise. Nor would you!

# The
# Stolen Shadow

Mark and Rachel were very happy. They were going for a picnic, and they had walked to Pixie Hill in the warm sunshine. Mark carried a bag in which was a bottle of lemonade, two apples and a book, and Rachel carried one with some sandwiches, two pieces of cake and a slab of chocolate.

"Isn't it fun to go off alone like this!" said Rachel. "Just ourselves – no one to say 'Don't!' No one to say 'Now mind you're good'."

"We'll have a picnic on the side of Pixie Hill," said Mark. "I'm getting hungry – aren't you? Wasn't it nice of Mummy to pack us such a lovely lunch!"

They went up the hill. There were gorse bushes there and soft heather.

Bracken grew around too, and a few pretty silver birches. Mark looked round for a nice place to sit.

"Look at that little clearing over there," he said, pointing to a round piece of grass under a silver birch. "Let's go there. If we sit in the heather we shan't be able to stand our lemonade bottle up properly."

They went to the round patch of grass and sat down. Soon they had spread out their feast and were busy eating it.

"Rachel!" said Mark, suddenly. "I thought I saw something moving in the heather over there. Maybe it was a bird or a rabbit – but it seemed to have a *face*!"

"Ooh! Was it a pixie, do you suppose?" said Rachel excitedly. "They were once believed to live on this hill, you know! Look again, Mark!"

"There it is!" said Mark, and he pointed. Rachel saw a mischievous little face peeping out of the heather. Then out hopped a small pixie, with a large pair of scissors!

"Good day to you," he said in a high, twittering voice, like a bird's. "Will you sell me something?"

"It depends what you want," said Mark, staring at the pixie in surprise.

"I want a shadow," said the pixie. "My master, the Enchanter Bushy-Brow, needs one to make a spell. So he has sent me out to buy a nice black shadow. I will give you one golden piece if I may cut off yours!"

"You can't cut a shadow off!" said Mark. "You know you can't!"

"You can't with ordinary scissors," said the pixie. "But you can with these.

They have been dipped in magic and can cut anything! Watch me cut this tree's shadow!"

He ran to where the shadow of the silver birch tree waved on the ground. He snipped with his scissors – and hey presto, they cut the shadow, and the pixie tossed it over to the astonished children.

"There you are!" he said. "What did I say?"

Rachel picked up the little shadow snippet. It was cold, light and soft and silky as spider thread. It was like nothing she had ever seen, and shone now purple, now black.

"Well!" she said. "This is very strange. But, pixie, I'm sorry, you can't possibly cut either of our shadows. We should hate to be without them. They follow us wherever we go. We shouldn't feel real without them, you know. Sometimes they are long, and sometimes they are short – but they are always there, as long as there is any daylight or light of any kind!"

The pixie looked sulky. He made a rude face at the children, hopped back into the heather and disappeared.

"I don't think I like that pixie much," said Rachel. "But fancy seeing one, Mark! How awfully exciting!"

"I wonder if he has a little house in that heather," said Mark. "Let's go and look."

The two children left the shade of the birch tree and went towards the heather. Their shadows stretched dark behind them, for the sun was very strong.

They peered down into the heather. They did not hear a tiny burst of

laughter, nor did they see the small pixie creeping behind them with his big scissors.

He ran to the edge of Rachel's short shadow. Snip-snip-snip went his scissors, and soon he had cut her shadow all round the edge!

Then he gave two sharp snips by her feet – and he had her shadow. Quick as lightning he rolled it up, tucked it under his arm, and fled off, laughing like a little waterfall.

Mark looked round at once, for he knew it was the pixie. "Look, Rachel, look!" he cried. "It's the pixie again! What's that he's got under his arm?"

"Oh, oh! It's my shadow!" said Rachel, looking down at her feet. "See, Mark, there's *your* shadow – but there isn't one for me. That horrid, horrid little thing snipped mine away when we were looking into the heather just now!"

"Oh, Rachel, how dreadful!" said Mark, staring down at Rachel's feet. "You do look strange without a shadow. Whatever shall we do?"

"We must get it back!" said Rachel, and she began to run after the pixie. "Come on, Mark, quick! I'm going to lose my shadow. Hurry!"

131

They tore off, and the running pixie heard them. He ran to a small yellow door set closely into the hillside, opened it, and disappeared. The door slammed.

"Quick! He's gone in here!" said Mark, and he banged at the door. It opened, and a rabbit looked out. She had a large apron on, and big glasses that kept slipping down her nose.

"Oh!" she said in surprise.

"Oh!" said both children, just as surprised.

"What do you want?" asked the rabbit. "First a pixie bursts into my house, slams the door and runs out the back way – and now you come banging. On my baking morning too!"

"So sorry!" said Mark, stepping inside. "But tell us where that pixie went. He's got my sister's shadow."

"Oh, the mischief," said the rabbit, putting her glasses on her forehead. "He's a rogue, he is. He came last week and wanted two of my whiskers for something, and the faces he made at me when I told him to grow some of his own, and cut those."

She shook her head and her glasses slid down her nose again. She pointed to her back door.

"He went out there," she said. "Hurry up, and you'll catch him!"

The children shot out of the door, and to their enormous surprise found themselves in a large open field, instead of inside the hill. They looked all about – but not a sign of the pixie was to be seen!

"Bother!" said Rachel. "Where's he gone?"

"To Bushy-Brow the Enchanter, I suppose!" said Mark gloomily. "We shall never get him now, Rachel. He has got too big a start, and we don't know which way he went."

"Well, we know where he's going, don't we!" said Rachel. "If we find the way to the Enchanter's, we might get there first, and stop him just as he's going in!"

"Good idea!" said Mark. "We'll ask the way, as soon as we see someone."

"Look, we'll ask this person," said Rachel. "He looks like a gnome." It *was* a gnome – he came shuffling over the field towards them, his long beard

nearly reaching the ground. He muttered something as he went, and the children felt half afraid of speaking to him.

"Threepence and twopence and a penny, how much change from tenpence?" they heard him say. "Threepence and twopence and a penny, how much —"

"The answer is fourpence," said Mark.

"Ooh!" said the gnome, startled. He stopped and stared at Mark. "Fourpence did you say? Ah, then I have the right change after all! I can cheer up! I thought I should have fivepence."

"Can you tell us where Bushy-Brow the Enchanter lives?" asked Mark, pleased to see the gnome smiling brightly.

"Certainly, certainly," said the gnome. "Do you see that hill over there? Go up it, take the mat at the top, slide to the bus, take the bus to the pond, hop on a duck and there you are!"

He went off, whistling cheerily.

"What funny directions," said Rachel, puzzled. "They sound quite mad to me."

"Well, I suppose this must be part of Fairyland," said Mark, "so we must expect funny things. Come on. Let's go up that hill and see if there really is a mat at the top."

"Slide to the bus, take the bus to the pond, hop on a duck and there you are!" repeated Rachel. "Well, it's easy enough to remember!"

They ran to the hill and began to climb up. It was steep and they puffed and panted. When they got to the top they exclaimed in delight – for below them lay Fairyland, smiling in the sun! Castles and palaces, crooked houses and toadstool villages spread before them. It was a marvellous sight!

The two children gazed for a long time and were too delighted to say a word. Then they looked for the runaway pixie – but he was nowhere to be seen.

"Oh, Rachel, here's the mat! Do come and look!" cried Mark. Rachel ran to him – and sure enough, there was a large blue mat, hanging on a peg – and stretching down the hill in front was a long, steep, slippery slide!

"We go down the slide on the mat!" said Mark. "Rachel, what fun!"

Before they could use the mat, a brownie came running up, unhitched the mat from the peg, set it at the top of

the slide, and down he went, his hair streaming out behind him.

"Oh, now he has taken the mat!" said Rachel in disappointment. The brownie reached the bottom, threw the mat into the air, and, to the children's great astonishment, it flew up the hill again on a pair of butterfly-like wings! It hung itself on the peg, and closed its wings tightly, so that they could hardly be seen.

"Quick, before anyone else takes it," said Mark. He caught up the mat and put it at the top of the slide. He and

Rachel got on, and pushed off. Whoooooooosh! Down flew the mat at top speed, right to the very bottom. It was a most exciting feeling.

"I wish we could do that again," said Mark, getting off. He threw the mat into the air, as he had seen the brownie do, and at once it spread its wings and flew up to the hilltop, where it once more hung itself up.

"Fairyland is much more exciting than *our* world!" said Rachel. "Come on. We must look for the bus."

"There it is, in front of you!" said Mark. "You don't need to look for it!"

"Oh, isn't it small!" cried Rachel, in delight. So it was – very small indeed. It was painted yellow, and had bright red wheels, so it was very colourful. There was no conductor and no driver, so the children wondered what to do.

A large fat rabbit walked by, wheeling a pram with six baby rabbits in. Mark ran up to her.

"Please, what time does the bus go?" he asked.

"Any time you like," said the rabbit, looking puzzled. "Just get in if you want to and drive off!"

"Oh! Do you mean *we* can drive it?" asked Rachel, in delight. "Well, where's the pond? We have to drive to that."

"Just say 'Pond' to the bus, and it'll know the way," said the rabbit. Two of her baby rabbits began to cry, so she hurriedly said goodbye and wheeled her pram away, saying: "Sh! Sh! Sh!"

"Isn't everything simply lovely here?" said Rachel. "I should be perfectly happy if only I had my shadow back again!"

They climbed in at the front of the bus. Mark took hold of the wooden steering-wheel, and said "Pond!" in his loudest voice. The bus shook itself, and began to trundle away down a narrow lane. It rumbled on for a long way, and at last ran down to a big pond. To the children's surprise it ran right into the water and floated towards some big ducks who were quacking together nearby.

When the ducks saw the children, two of them swam up at once. Mark and Rachel stepped neatly on to their backs, and the bus floated back to the bank. It got out, shook itself, and trundled back up the lane, gleaming in the sun. It was really a very good and clever little bus. The children felt quite sorry to see it go.

"Take us to Bushy-Brow the Enchanter," said Mark to the duck.

"Quark!" said the duck, in a deep voice. "Quark, quark!"

Instead of swimming, the ducks suddenly spread out big white wings and rose into the air. The children were

141

so astonished, that they nearly fell off! Mark half slid off, and then, catching tight hold of the duck's neck, he pulled himself up again.

"Quark!" said the duck severely. "If you do that sort of thing I shall choke! I could hardly breathe then."

"So sorry," said Mark humbly. He and Rachel sat very still after that, and looked down on the palaces and castles of Fairyland as they flew over them. At last the duck flew down to a strange tower-like house, set on the top of a hill.

"Quark!" said one of the ducks. "Here you are!"

The children slipped off their feathery backs and looked at the tower-like building. The ducks flew away and left them there.

"How do we get in?" said Mark puzzled. "There isn't any door!"

There certainly didn't seem to be! The children walked round and round – but no, not even the tiniest door was to be seen! Then they suddenly saw one!

It appeared before their very eyes – a

bright blue one with a brass knocker! It opened – and out shot, who do you think? Yes – that mischievous pixie who had taken Rachel's shadow.

Someone kicked him out – and at the same time an angry voice cried: "You meddlesome creature, you! You've spoilt my spell!"

Then the door shut – and immediately vanished again! The pixie sat up and began to cry. But as soon as he saw Mark and Rachel, he looked most astonished and stopped.

"How did you get here?" he asked.

"Never mind that!" said Mark in a cross voice. "Tell me this – where's my sister's shadow that you stole, you wicked little creature?"

"Bushy-Brow has got it!" said the pixie with a grin. Mark looked so angry that his grin stopped and he jumped to his feet. Mark shot out his hand to get hold of him – but he dodged away, shouting: "Can't catch *me*, can't catch *me*!"

"Let him be," said Rachel in disgust. "He is a most tiresome little fellow – but he hasn't got my shadow now, that's plain. Let's bang on the place where the door was, and see if we can get the Enchanter to speak to us."

So they went to where the door had been and banged hard. A cross voice came from inside.

"If that's you again, pixie, I'll turn you into birdseed and give you to my canary!"

"It isn't the pixie," said Mark. "It's two children come to see you."

At once the blue door appeared again, and was thrown open. The children saw a tall, kindly-faced old man, wearing an enormous pointed hat, and a curious black cloak that flowed round him like water.

"This is an honour and a pleasure!" he said. "I don't often have children to visit me! Come in!"

The children went inside the tower-house. It was small inside, but the ceiling was so high that they couldn't reach it. A fire burned in one corner and in the middle of the floor was a deep hole out of which came a bubbling noise and some strange yellow mist.

"Don't be frightened," said Bushy-Brow. "That's only where I make my spells,"

"Oh," said Mark, "isn't it strange."

"It may be strange to *you*," said Bushy-Brow politely, "but quite ordinary to *me*."

He smiled at Mark, and then stared hard at Rachel. He stared so hard that the little girl felt most uncomfortable. He looked at her feet, he looked at her face, then he looked back at her feet again.

"Little girl," he said in a puzzled

voice, "there is something very strange about you – you have no shadow! Did you know this?"

"Oh, yes," said Rachel. "Of course I know. That wicked little pixie of yours stole it from me this morning. He snipped it off with his scissors!"

"Stars and moon! So it was *your* shadow he brought," cried Bushy-Brow. "He told me it was the shadow of an old woman who didn't want hers any more. The naughty little creature! I'll certainly turn him into birdseed."

"Oh, no, don't do that!" said Rachel. "I really shouldn't like you to do that, although I don't like the pixie a bit. But I *would* like my shadow back, please!"

"My dear little girl, I've used it in that spell you see being made at this very minute!" said the Enchanter, and he pointed to where the strange yellow mist came up from the bubbling hole in the floor.

"Oh, I say! *Now* what shall I do?" said poor Rachel, with tears in her eyes. "I *must* have a shadow!"

"You shall have one!" said Bushy-Brow, patting her on the back, kindly. "Don't cry! I wouldn't have used your shadow for worlds, if I'd known it was yours."

He went to the door and stared out. "Pippetty, Pippetty!" he called. "Come here! I want you!"

The naughty little pixie came running up. The Enchanter took hold of him and marched him into the tall room.

"This little girl says you took her shadow," he said sternly. "I have used it in my spell, thinking it was an old woman's. You are a wicked fellow, Pippetty. I shall take away *your* shadow and give it to this little girl!"

The pixie began to cry, but it was no use. The Enchanter took some big

scissors and neatly snipped away all the pixie's purple-black shadow. Then he smacked him and sent him outside, looking very strange without his shadow!

The Enchanter took a needle and threaded it with purple silk. Then he picked up the shadow and went to Rachel.

"Oh dear, are you going to sew it on me?" said the little girl, frightened. "Will it hurt?"

"Not a bit!" said Bushy-Brow. He dug the needle into his hand, and then into Rachel – she couldn't feel the slightest prick!

149

"It's magic!" he said.

He bent down and swiftly sewed the little shadow to Rachel's feet, watered it with something from a can, and then muttered some strange words. The shadow stretched itself, shivered a bit, and then lay still.

"It's yours now," said the Enchanter. "A bit small for you, perhaps – but no one will notice. Once a year, on Midsummer's Night, it will try to get away from you to go to the pixies' ball, but just wish a wish, and it will be still again."

"Wish a wish!" said Rachel in delight. "Will it come true?"

"Of course," said the Enchanter. "Try a wish now, if you like, and see."

"I wish we were home!" said Rachel,

150

at once – and hey presto, there came an enormous wind that caught them up, twisted them round seven times and set them down again – in their very own garden! What do you think of that?

"I can't believe it!" cried Rachel.

"Oh, Rachel, why did you wish us away?" said Mark. "We were having such a great time!"

"Never mind! I've got one wish every year!" said Rachel. "I'll wish us back again, if you like, next Midsummer's Night! Oh, what fun! I'm glad, glad, glad I've got a pixie-shadow instead of my own!"

"You must be the only girl in the world who has!" said Mark. "I wish I had too!"

"Perhaps I'll wish one for you too, one year," said Rachel. "Come on – let's go and tell Mummy all about it!"

They did – and Mummy said yes, it was perfectly true, Rachel's shadow *was* small for her – and the shadow's ears always looked pointed, like a pixie's. Isn't it strange?

# The Voice
# in The Shed

The new gardener wasn't at all nice. The children didn't like him a bit. "He shouts at me," said Ann. "Even if I'm only just walking down the path he shouts at me."

"And he told me he'd put my wheelbarrow on his bonfire if I left it out in the garden again," said John.

"And today he said we weren't to go into the shed any more," said Peter. "Why, we've *always* been allowed in the shed, ever since we can remember. It's our shed, not his."

"Does he think we'll break his tools or something?" said Ann. "We shouldn't. Anyway, they are mostly Daddy's tools, not his."

"I shall tell Daddy I don't like him," said John.

But Daddy only laughed. "Old Mr Jacks let you do anything you liked."

"Mr Jacks was nice," said Ann. "I liked him. He gave me strawberry plants for my garden."

"This new man, Mr Tanner, is a very good gardener," said Daddy. "Much better than old Jacks was. Maybe he thinks you children will run over his seed-beds or something. Keep out of his way."

But they couldn't very well keep out of Mr Tanner's way, because, after all, they had to play in the garden – and, except for Sundays, Mr Tanner was always there, keeping a look-out for them.

153

He ordered them off whenever he came across them. He grumbled if they dared to pick anything. But he was crossest of all if he caught them in the garden-shed.

"You're not to go in there," he stormed. "How many times do I have to tell you? I keep my things in there and I'm not having a lot of children messing about with them. You keep out."

"But we've *always* played in the shed if we wanted to," said John, boldly.

"Well, you won't any more," said Mr Tanner, disagreeably. "I'll lock it, see?"

He not only locked it, he frightened Ann and Peter very much. He caught

them peeping in at the shed window one day and he yelled at them so crossly that they almost fell off the water-butt in fright.

"You be careful," he said. "I'm going to put someone in there to scare you out! See? You be careful."

"Who?" asked Ann, fearfully.

"Ah – you wait and see," said Mr Tanner. "I'll have my Someone there very soon – and won't he chase you when you come messing around!"

Ann and Peter didn't like this idea at all. Who was this horrid Someone? Ann dreamt about it at night, and told John. He was the oldest of the three and he laughed.

"It's only something that Mr Tanner has made up to scare you," he said. "He hasn't got a Someone."

But Ann and Peter didn't believe John. They were quite sure that Mr Tanner was horrid enough to keep a strange Someone in their garden shed to scare them away. They didn't go near the shed after that.

"You shouldn't scare my sister and brother like that," said John boldly to Mr Tanner. "It's wrong."

"You get away," said Mr Tanner, in his surly voice. "I'll do as I like. Pests of children you are. I never did like a place with kids about."

John went off. He was angry. How dare old Tanner scare Ann and Peter? He went to call on his friend Tom, who lived just down the road. He told Tom all about it.

Tom listened. "Does Mr Tanner have his dinner in that shed?" he asked.

"Yes. Why?" asked John.

"Well, I've got an idea," said Tom. "What about *us* putting a Someone in that shed – a Someone who'll scare old Tanner stiff?"

"How can we do that?" asked John, in wonder.

"Well, listen," said Tom. "You know my mother's parrot, don't you? He says all kinds of things in that funny, hollow voice of his. Couldn't we stick him in the shed somewhere and hide him?

156

He'll talk as soon as old Tanner goes in – and what a fright he'll get when he hears a voice and can't see anyone who owns it!"

John was thrilled. "But what would your mother say if your parrot isn't here at home?" he asked.

"Mother's away for a few days," said Tom. "Old Mr Polly, our parrot, won't mind where we put him so long as he has plenty of sunflower seeds to eat. Anyway, we can always go and take him out of the shed when Mr Tanner has gone at five o'clock."

So that was how old Mr Polly, Tom's parrot, came to be hidden inside the garden shed. He was put there in his big cage, with plenty of food and water. One

side of the cage was covered with a sack to hide it.

"Now then you, now then," remarked Mr Polly, in a curious hoarse voice as the boys arranged his cage in the shed. He coughed in a nasty hollow way. "Fetch a doctor. A-tish-OOOO!"

He gave such a life-like sneeze that John jumped. Tom giggled. "It's all right. He's full of silly ways and sayings. Hasn't he got a lovely voice! My word, he'll make Mr Tanner jump!"

The next day Mr Tanner saw John near the garden shed with Peter, and he spoke to them sharply. "What did I tell you? Clear off – or the Someone in that shed will get you!"

Peter ran off, looking scared. John spoke up at once.

"You're right, Mr Tanner. There *is* a Someone in the shed. I heard his voice – a deep, hollow kind of voice. I wonder you're not scared, too."

"Aha," said Mr Tanner, "what did I say? You be careful of that shed!"

The parrot in the shed coughed

solemnly. The sound came out to where Mr Tanner stood with John. He looked a little startled.

"There," said John, cocking his head on one side. "Your Someone is coughing. Why don't you give him some cough medicine?"

"It's only the old gardener in the next-door garden," said Mr Tanner, and drove his fork into the ground. "You clear off."

Old Mr Polly began to whistle a mournful tune inside the shed.

"Hear that?" said John. "Your Someone is whistling now. You really *have* got a Someone there, haven't you? Aren't you scared, too?"

159

"I told you to clear off," said Mr Tanner, looking rather uneasy. John grinned and went off, very pleased with himself.

Mr Tanner couldn't imagine where the curious noises were coming from that morning. Once he heard a voice – a deep, solemn voice. It certainly sounded as if it came from the shed. Another time he heard a cough, and yet another time a sneeze. Yet, when he went and looked into the shed there was nobody there.

John went to tell Ann and Peter what he and Tom had done. They listened in amazement. Peter laughed. "I'm glad. Let's go and take our lunch near the shed today if Mother will let us – then we can see what happens."

So they took a picnic lunch to the back of the shed as soon as Mr Tanner had gone inside to eat *his* lunch!

Mr Tanner opened his lunch packet. He was just about to take up a cheese sandwich when a hollow voice spoke loudly and solemnly.

"There's NO rest for the wicked. Ah me, ah me! Fetch a doctor!"

Mr Tanner was so startled that he dropped his sandwich on the floor. He turned round to see who had spoken, but there was nobody there.

It must be somebody outside the shed! Mr Tanner picked up his sandwich and began to eat it.

The voice began again. "See, saw, Margery daw, see saw, saw see, see saw, saw see ..."

Mr Tanner began to tremble. He dropped his sandwich again.

"Who's there?" he said in a shaky voice. "Who is it?"

"Here comes a candle to light you to bed, here comes a CHOPPER!" shouted the voice very suddenly, and gave a

dreadful squawk that made Mr Tanner leap to his feet in fright, half expecting to see a candle and a chopper coming at him from somewhere.

"Who are you?" cried Mr Tanner, and jumped as John came to the door of the shed. John had heard all this and was thrilled. He looked at the frightened gardener.

"Is that your Someone talking to you?" he asked. "Why do you look so afraid? It's *your* Someone, isn't it?"

Old Mr Polly took it into his head at that moment to give an imitation of an aeroplane coming down low. He always did this extremely well, and it scared

poor old Tanner almost out of his life. It even startled John. Mr Tanner stumbled over a few pots and fled out of the door into the bright sunshine. He was trembling all over.

"I can't go in there again," he told John. "You fetch out my tools for me. I'm going."

And when John gave him the few tools that belonged to him, off he went, looking very pale.

The children watched him go, feeling pleased. "His Someone came to life and frightened him!" said John, with a grin. "I'll go and get Tom and we'll carry old Mr Polly back home again. Good Mr Polly – he acted well! My word, did you hear him imitate an aeroplane?"

Mr Polly obligingly did it again. It was wonderful! John pulled the sacking off his cage, and the three children stood and watched the old parrot admiringly.

"What will Daddy say when he hears Mr Tanner has gone?" asked Ann.

Daddy was glad! "I've heard bad things about that fellow the last day or two!" he said. "Very bad. He isn't honest, for one thing. I'm glad he's gone. I'll get old Mr Jacks back again. He's not so good a gardener, but he's absolutely honest and trustworthy."

"Oh, *good*!" said all the children. "We do like Mr Jacks."

And back came old Mr Jacks, beaming all over his face. "Well, I'm downright pleased to see you all again," he said. "I can't think why that fellow Tanner went

off as he did. Do you know
me?"

"No – what?" asked John.

"He told me not to go into
shed!" said old Mr Jacks, wit        of
laughter. "Said there was a Voice there
that frightened him away. A *Voice*! Did
you ever hear of such a thing? Is there a
Voice there, John? What do you say to
that?"

"No, there isn't any Voice there – not
now old Tanner's gone, anyway," said
John, and he laughed. "He scared us by
telling us he kept a Someone there, Mr
Jacks – but when his Someone grew a
voice he didn't like it. He ran away."

"What tales you tell!" said Mr Jacks,
not believing a word. "Well, Voice or no
Voice, I'm having my dinner in that
shed as usual every day – and, what's
more, you can come and share it
whenever you like."

"Thank you!" said all three, joyfully.
So they often do – but they've none of
them heard that Voice again! It isn't
really very surprising, is it?

# What a Peculiar Thing!

Peter had a lot of money in his pockets. He had seen his Uncle Ben the day before, and Uncle Ben had been very generous indeed.

"Here you are," he said. "Four pounds for you to spend! Catch!" And he threw four pound coins over to Peter. How rich he felt.

Well, Peter spent it all. He bought three bars of chocolate, a bag of sweets, a box of marbles, a fine pencil, a very large magnet that could attract all kinds of things to it, and a splendid knife.

He showed the things to everyone when he got to school, taking them out of his blazer pockets one after another. The boys stared in astonishment, and the girls looked longingly at the chocolate.

"Aren't I lucky?" said Peter. "Did you ever see such a fine lot of marbles? And look how well this pencil writes. And do you see all the blades in this knife?"

"What's in the bag?" asked Rosie. She knew it was sweets, of course. But Peter was mean with sweets. Rosie thought he might offer them round if she spoke about them.

But he didn't. Instead he took out a bar of chocolate and broke it into tiny bits. He gave everyone a very, very small piece indeed. They looked at one another.

167

"Isn't he a meanie?" whispered Hettie. "I can hardly taste my bit!" Rosie spoke out loudly. "What about a sweet, Peter? And what about letting us try your pencil and your magnet and play with those lovely marbles?"

"I'll see," said Peter. "It's almost school-time now."

"What you really mean is – you jolly well don't mean to let us share in any of your good luck except to have a crumb of chocolate," said Rosie. "You be careful, Peter – you might lose all those things – they might suddenly disappear and vanish into thin air!"

"Pooh! You've been reading fairy stories," said Peter. "Things like that don't happen in real life, as you very well know."

Rosie was right. He didn't mean to share anything else. He didn't mean to let the others play with his new things. He wanted them all to himself.

Nobody said anything more to him that morning. They knew Peter! They wouldn't get a sweet from him, or any more chocolate; they wouldn't even be allowed to roll a marble!

Peter always went home by bus. Some of the other boys went home by bus, too. If Peter hadn't been so lost in thinking of his new possessions that morning he would have noticed the boys putting their head together and making a little plan! But he didn't notice. He didn't see that somebody took his blazer from its peg and put someone else's in its place.

He didn't notice something being stuffed into that blazer's pockets! He put it on, and ran off to catch the bus with the others.

When he was sitting down in the bus he put his hand into his pocket to feel his new things. He felt about for his marbles. Where were they?

He felt something hard and round and pulled it out. Goodness! What a dirty, chipped thing! Where could it have come from? And here was another and another – horrible, cheap little marbles! Where were his own?

He felt in his other pocket. The boys watched him, nudging each other, and giggled. Peter brought out a magnet – but not his beautiful big one! This was a misery of a magnet, thin and light. Peter began to feel alarmed.

"What's happened?" he thought, and he felt desperately in his pockets for his bars of chocolate. He brought out a bit of chocolate paper wrapped round a rather dirty bit of chocolate – there were no bars at all!

"What else did I have?" thought Peter, most alarmed. "Oh – my pocketknife. Surely that's here!"

But it wasn't. All he found was a little broken knife with one poor blade! He felt very upset indeed. Even his sweets were gone – there were only two or three empty sweet wrappings. And what about his new pencil? He groped in alarm for it – and brought out a little

171

yellow stump of pencil with a broken point!

His heart sank. He remembered what Rosie had said. His new things might disappear into thin air! They seemed not only to have disappeared but to have exchanged themselves for the same kind of things – but how different! He looked at the poor little knife and pencil, really scared.

"Hey, Peter – you get out here!" called Harry. Peter shot out of the bus, not seeing the boys' grins. They looked at one another and laughed.

"He can't understand what's happened!" said Harry. "Well, this

172

afternoon we'll change the blazers again, so that he gets his own, with everything in it. We'll see if he's learnt his lesson!"

Poor Peter! He really was miserable. He didn't like to tell his mother about the odd things that seemed to have happened to his things. He went back to school that afternoon very quiet indeed.

"Hello!" said Harry. "Got your new marbles with you, Peter? Let's have a look at them again!" Peter looked at Harry. Then he pulled out the little miseries of marbles and held them out.

"Look," he said. "See what's happened to my beauties! I boasted I wouldn't share them – and now something's happened to everything I had."

"Bad luck," said Rosie, who was in the secret. "I bet you wish you'd got all your things back again, don't you? Gracious – look at your knife – and the pencil! How they've changed! You shouldn't have been so mean."

"I'd share *everything* if only they'd

change back to what they were," said Peter, gloomily. The girls and boys looked at one another. Ah – *would* he? They would see! Peter put his right blazer on after afternoon school. It had been put back on his peg. He stuffed his hands into his pockets – and a most amazed look came over his face. Good gracious! Two bars of chocolate – a bag of sweets – an enormous magnet – a fine pencil – and a beautiful penknife – and here were his marbles, just as big as ever!

"Why – they're all right again," said Peter, astonished. He looked round at the laughing children. "Oh – you horrid things – you played a trick on me – you changed my blazer! I know you did. Why did you?"

"Just to teach you something, Peter," said Rosie. "But we don't know yet whether we *have* managed to teach you."

Peter went red. He looked at Harry, who grinned. He looked at Rosie and all the rest. Then he held out the bag of sweets.

"Have one, all of you," he said. "And we'll share the chocolate, too."

"Hurrah! He's a sport!" cried Rosie, and she clapped him on the back.

"Good old Peter. He's a sport, after all!" So he was – but he very nearly wasn't! It was a funny joke to play, wasn't it? But a very good one!

# What's Happened to Michael?

"I've got four pounds and fifty pence saved up for Christmas presents already," said Jane, counting out coins from her money-box.

"I've got three pounds exactly," said Peter. "I had to give fifty pence in at school for Miss Brown's wedding present. How much have *you* got, Michael?"

"Not much," said Michael, and he shook his money-box out on the table. A twenty pence piece rolled out. "Twenty pence! But I just can't bother to save!"

"I think you're mean," said Jane. "You never save up to buy people birthday presents or Christmas presents. You just give them old toys of yours. You spend all your money on yourself, and you don't try to earn any to save up, as we do!"

"He's lazy," said Peter. "He won't put himself out for anyone. Will you, Michael? You'll let us spend our saved-up money to buy you a Christmas present – but you wouldn't dream of doing the same for us."

"Oh, be quiet," said Michael. "We can't all be the same. I don't want to bother to earn money, and I don't want to bother to save. You like it and I don't."

He went out of the room and banged the door.

"He really is mean," said Jane. "He never even bought Mummy a birthday present on her last birthday. He just went and picked some flowers out of the garden for her."

"Well – I don't expect he'll ever be different," said Peter. "He just doesn't care."

"There's one good thing about him though," said Jane. "He never borrows from us. Not like Tina at school, who's always borrowing something or other."

"And he'd never dream of taking any money that belonged to anyone else," said Peter. "Like that horrid little James at school. *He* took Harry's bus-money, you know – out of his desk. John saw him and made him put it back."

"Yes – thank goodness Michael isn't a borrower or a stealer," said Jane. "He's just careless, and rather mean. He hardly ever gives anyone a present."

Michael was out in the garden, looking for a ball he had lost. He thought of Jane and Peter and the money in their money-boxes. He

scowled to himself. All this fuss about saving up money to spend on other people! Birthdays and Christmases were a nuisance. There were quite enough things to buy without having to go and spend money on presents!

"I've got twenty pence – and as far as I can see that's about all I *shall* have to spend at Christmas-time on Mummy and Daddy and Jane and Peter," thought Michael, hunting under the bushes for his ball. "Five pence for each of them. I'll get them a card between them."

Next day Mummy came into the playroom where the three children were reading. "Will one of you go down to the village for me and fetch me some buns for tea?" she said. "I meant to make some and I haven't had time."

"I'll go," said Michael. "I've got to fetch my bike. It's at Fred's. I lent it to him."

"Very well," said his mother. "Here is a pound, Michael. Choose six nice buns. And will you go to the milk shop next door to the baker's and pay the bill for me? Here it is. Exactly five pounds. I'll give you a five pound note for it. Put the pound and the note carefully into your purse. Bring back the bill with you, and see that the girl receipts it, so that I know it's paid."

"Right, Mummy," said Michael, and took the pound and the five pound note. He felt in his pocket for his purse, but it wasn't there. Bother! Where was it?

Well, he would put the money into his pocket just as it was. He wouldn't have it there long!

He put on his hat and coat and went out, whistling. It was snowing hard, and he was pleased. He liked going out in the snow. Big snowflakes fell down all round him. He looked up into the heavy sky. Thousands of flakes were falling silently down and down and down. They gave him a pleasant but rather strange feeling.

He shuffled through the snow to his front gate. Then out into the road he went. He fetched his bike from Fred's first, but he couldn't ride it because already the snow was thick. He wheeled it to the baker's and stood looking into the shop. What buns should he buy? There were three different kinds. He would get two of each.

181

In he went and the girl put six buns into a paper bag. He gave her the pound and went out to his bike. Now, what else did Mummy say he was to do? Oh yes – pay the milk bill. He felt in his pocket for the bill and pulled it out. It was for five pounds. He would give in the five pound note, watch the girl write "Received with thanks" across the bill, and go home. Tomorrow he would make Jane and Peter come into the garden and build a snowman.

He went into the milk shop. He felt in his pocket for the five pound note. It wasn't there! He scrabbled hurriedly in all his pockets, one after another – but he couldn't find that note!

He went out of the shop before the girl came to serve him. He was very upset. What had happened to that five pounds? It was a lot of money. He felt in all his pockets again, very, very carefully. But, quite certainly, the five pound note wasn't there. Michael emptied out his pockets, laying everything on the top of the snow-covered wall nearby. String.

Two toffees. A small ball. A pencil. A rubber. A big marble. But no five pound note.

"I've dropped it somewhere," thought Michael, and he went back to the baker's. No, he hadn't dropped it there. The shop was empty, and there was nothing on the floor. There was nothing in the snow outside, either.

"The snow must have covered it," said Michael. "I dropped it somewhere and the snow hid it. Blow, bother, blow! A whole five pound note. Mummy will be awfully upset. I know she's saving up for Christmas, too – for crackers and balloons and things."

He wheeled his bicycle home, feeling very miserable. Mummy had told him to put the note in his purse. It was so easy to lose loose money. What should he say to her? If she told Daddy Michael would be sent to bed. Daddy didn't like carelessness with other people's money.

"I can't even give Mummy anything out of my money-box to make up for losing the five pounds," thought Michael. "I've only got twenty pence."

He wheeled his bicycle up the hill to his house, thinking hard. "Suppose I try and earn some money – perhaps I might even get five pounds if I tried! Then I

could go and pay the milk bill and nobody would know I'd lost Mummy's money. The milk shop won't send the bill in again for another week, so I've got a week. I could try, anyway. It would be difficult, I expect, to earn such a lot of money."

He put his bicycle away and went indoors. He was met by his mother, who held out her hand for the buns. "Put my milk bill receipt in my desk, Michael," she said. "What nice buns! Tea will be ready in five minutes. Tell the others, dear."

Michael went to tell Jane and Peter. They were still counting their money and making out Christmas lists of presents. "I haven't got enough money yet," said Jane. "I must somehow earn two pounds more."

"I must get a bit more too," said Peter. "Hallo, Michael. You've been ages." Michael looked at the little piles of money and wished he had as much. "How are you going to earn any more?" he asked.

"Well, I know what *I* shall do," said Peter. "I shall dig away the snow from people's front paths. They always pay for that."

"And I shall go and ask Mrs Johns if she wants me to take her two little children for a walk in the afternoons," said Jane. "And I could ask Auntie Nora if she wants any errands running. She knows I'm saving up for Christmas and she pays me twenty pence a time. I've told her I'll always do her errands for nothing if I'm not saving up."

Michael made up his mind to go and ask Granny if she wanted any errands running. And he would take his spade and broom and do a little snow-moving too! And what about cleaning Uncle Dick's car? Uncle Dick had once said jokingly that he would give the children a pound if any of them would like to clean his car. But it was such a big job that no one had taken it on.

Nobody could make out what had happened to Michael the next few days. He shovelled snow away from this house

and that house. He ran all Granny's errands quickly and well. He appeared at Uncle Dick's house and asked if he could clean the car.

"A pound to you if you do it well," said Uncle Dick, pleased to see that it was Michael who had offered to do it. He had always thought that Michael was the lazy one of the three.

Mummy was astonished to hear what Michael was doing. Granny praised him and said how good and quick he was. Uncle Dick said he had never had his car cleaned so well, and he gave Michael one pound fifty instead of a pound. Mrs

**188**

Brown and Miss Toms told Mummy how well Michael had shovelled the snow from their front doors.

"What's *happened* to Michael?" she said, in wonder. The other two children said the same, two or three times a day. "What's happened to Michael? He must be saving up for Christmas after all! He's earning a lot of money! We'll get presents from him if we're lucky."

Michael didn't say he was saving up for Christmas, because he wasn't. He was trying to earn money to pay for the milk bill, to make up for the five pounds he had lost. He emptied his money-box one night and counted out what he had got.

"Three pounds. Two fifty pence pieces. Three twenty pence pieces, counting the one I had before, and five ten pence pieces. Now, let's add them all up."

Have *you* added them up? You have? Well, then, you know what they come to – five pounds and ten pence! What a lot of money!

"Now I can pay that milk bill," said Michael, pleased. And just at that very minute in came his mother. She held something in her hand.

"Look, Michael," she said. "I was sending your old blazer to the cleaners and I went through the pockets. There was a hole in one pocket and this had slipped through it and was down in the lining – a five pound note! Where *did* you get it?"

Michael stood and stared at the note. Good gracious! So he *hadn't* lost it after all – it had slipped down into the lining. There it was!

"Oh, Mummy," he said. "I'll tell you what happened. I should have told you before, I know. You gave me that note to pay the milk bill – and I thought I had lost it; I didn't know it had slipped down into the lining. So I couldn't pay the bill and I've been hard at work earning money all this week to pay the milk bill myself. And now look at what I've earned! I've got five pounds and ten pence in my money-box!"

"Oh, Mike!" said his mother, astonished. "You should have told me at

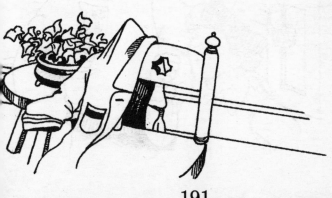

once and I would have looked in the lining and found the note. But as it is you've now got this note to pay the bill – and all that money besides!"

"To spend on Christmas presents," said Michael. "Yes, that's what I shall do. I've saved up like the others – and I'll make a fine Christmas list!"

Well, he did. He put down all the names of the people he wanted to give presents to, and beside the names he put the things he meant to buy. What a wonderful day of shopping he would have – and how pleased everyone would be with their presents! They were, of course – and it was very nice for Michael to hear their thanks. It was the happiest Christmas he had ever had. But wasn't it funny that a five pound note should cause all that?